A Merry Kin

A Merry Kin

Do Nonie

Oral Husemoen McDanel

Oral Husemoen McDanel

To order additional copies of this book, contact:
Xlibris Corporation
1-888-795-4274
www.Xlibris.com
Orders@Xlibris.com
24393

To my daughter Patricia without whose help and encouragement this book would never have been written.

And to my sister Joyce, "Iggy Wando Iffel Giffel"

CHAPTER ONE

Suzy Q was different. She was different from other children in many ways. For starters she was very tiny and she was the only first grader completely happy on starting school. She paid no attention to what the other little girls owned or what they did, she was happy with herself. She also felt different but knew some day she would understand why. She spent a lot of her time daydreaming of some far off day she called "that day". It would be the day when her world would change and she would have her very own family.

Suzy Q was an orphan. Her full name was Susanna Isabel Amanda Kinsraldo or so it said on the slip of paper fastened to her bunting when she was found, all alone, in a small house on the outskirts of a small town on the Olympic peninsula.

Two teenagers who were out hiking had heard crying in an empty house. They had looked in a window, saw a baby lying on a small rug in an otherwise empty room and believing no one else was in the house they went inside. They were right, the house was empty so they took the baby and carried it to the police chief. Everyone in the small town was questioned, but no one had ever heard of the unusual name Kinsraldo and therefore no one knew whom she could belong to or where she came from. The town people only knew that the house once belonged to a doctor and taxes on the house were still being paid. Everyone decided there was no connection between house and child as the names were different.

In due time she was given to Mr. And Mrs. Haveahorde who took care of all the orphans of the county. They were nice people but just had too many children to care for and too much to do, so mostly the children took care of each other. Bernie and Muffin Haveahorde spent most of their time cooking for the dozen or so children. No one was sure how many there were and there was never enough time to do all the necessary work it took to care for so many. The clothes washing never seemed to get done and baths and clean clothes for school were often missing. Suzy Q never thought about all this until the day she started first grade. It was terrible. The other girl who was supposed to get her properly washed and dressed was too busy worrying about her own looks to pay any attention to Suzy Q. Suzy Q. did her best to find something to wear and washed her face and combed her hair but alas she was only five and a half so she didn't do a very good job of it. There were so many children leaving at once for school that Ma and Pa H, as the children called them, over looked Suzy Q's grooming.

She arrived at school with uncombed hair, different colored socks and a skirt she had to safety pin to her blouse so it wouldn't fall off. The other first graders laughed and pointed at her until she just wanted to hide. She tried to remember her dream of "that day" and to stay happy, but when the other children started teasing her it was just too much to bear. She would have ran back home but just then, the teacher, who had pretty twinkle eyes, saw what was happening and came and took her hand. She led all the children to their classroom and took Suzy Q to a desk in the front row.

Miss Twinkle-eyes asked each child their name and when Suzy Q answered, "Suzy Q," the children all laughed again, calling it a funny name or really not a name at all.

Suzy Q was really upset and wasn't going to explain why she was called Suzy Q, but then without asking the teacher, she stood up, turned around and looking at the girls who had done the finger pointing in the school yard and laughed the most, she said, "My name is really Princess Susanna Isabel Amanda Kinsraldo" but my name is so long I prefer to be known as Suzy Q".

Why she said Princess she would never know, it just popped into her head. She would never tell them that when she first learned her full name she had called herself Suzy. The older children at the Haveahordes had added the Q because she was always asking questions. She turned back toward the front of the class and sat down at her desk.

Miss Twinkle-eyes smiled at her and said, "Thank you, I will call you Suzy Q as your prefer."

The rest of the day went well except for recesses. The same little girl whose name was Veronica, kept making unkind remarks about Suzy Q's looks. Veronica had curly hair and wore, of all things, a blue silk dress. She was kind of pretty, Suzy Q thought, but at recesses and noon she would act bossy telling the other girls, who followed her, what they should do. Most of the other girls wore jeans or pants and Suzy Q decided that from now on she would too, as there was always lots of jeans and overalls given to the Haveahordes and not many dresses.

Soon school was over for the day and Suzy Q ran as fast as she could for home.

CHAPTER TWO

The next two years went by rather well for Suzy Q as long as she could avoid Veronica, outside of the schoolroom. It was really hard as Veronica was always hunting for her so she could say mean things. Suzy Q was a very good student and made A's in all subjects. Suzy Q had also learned from her teacher how to brush her long wavy brown hair so it looked nice and she tied it in a ponytail to keep it neat. Her teacher gave her a pretty red ribbon for her hair. She also had learned to bathe without being reminded to and brush her teeth each day. Maybe her overalls weren't the nicest of clothes but now they were always clean even if she had to wash them herself.

Suzy Q had acquired lots of friends and it was more than Veronica could stand, so she tried to dream up ideas to hurt Suzy Q.

The one thing that hurt Suzy Q the most was Veronica's constant teasing about her size. Everyday when Suzy Q went to school, Veronica was waiting so she could sing the song she had made up. Suzy Q even dreaded recess for she knew she would again hear Veronica sing, "Tiny little Suzy Q, small as a baby, Boo Hoo Hoo!" This always made Veronica's friends laugh, even though they had heard the stupid song tons of times. Suzy Q always felt like crying, but she always held the tears back while she rushed over to her good friends. Her playmates would quickly start a game to distract Suzy Q. She never told her friends that she was worried sick because she wasn't growing and the song hurt so much because Veronica was right, she was tiny!

The Haveahordes had a place on their kitchen wall where all the children's height was measured every six months. In two years

Suzy Q had only grown one quarter of an inch. She was the only one who hadn't added two or three inches in that time. She stuffed her self with food, stretched herself by hanging on the playground bars, but nothing helped. If she didn't grow soon, she wondered how much longer her friends would defy Veronica and choose her to play on their side in games.

CHAPTER THREE

Veronica knew that the orphans never had many toys or dolls so she had an idea. She knew she needed her mother's help for she would have to include the boys or some one might figure what she wanted to do wasn't fair. That weekend she worked on her idea. The Hobnobs, Veronica's parents, were very wealthy and had a beautiful big house with a very large yard, with lots of lawn bordered by flowers. It was a perfect place for a party.

In a week spring vacation would start. Saturday, before that week, Veronica moped around till her mother asked her why she looked so unhappy. Veronica said that she was thinking about spring vacation, in a week, with nothing to do.

"Well," her mother said, "Maybe we could have a party on the lawn Saturday, the first day of vacation, if the weather is nice".

Veronica was tickled pink, she knew her mother would offer a party, as it was always Mrs. Hobnobs cure for being unhappy. Now Veronica had to be careful so her Mother would think every thing was her idea. Veronica asked if the party was going to be for all of the children in her room.

"But of course," said Mrs. Hobnob.

As Mini Creek was such a small town there were only 22 children in the three grades and they all shared the same schoolroom.

"What will we do all afternoon?" asked Veronica.

"You could play games" her mother replied.

"That's so dull and we do it at school all the time," whined Veronica, then she continued, "If we could only have some kind of toy contest with a prize."

"That's just what I was thinking, you must have read my mind", exclaimed her Mother, and then continued "we will have a prize for the girls and one for the boys. All boys have toy cars and all girls have dolls so we will give a prize for the best-kept car for the boys and the nicest doll for the girls."

"How wonderful" said Veronica, "And will you come to school Monday and tell the teacher so we can have all week to fix up our doll?"

To this Veronica's Mother had agreed and now Veronica had just the kind of party and contest she wanted, for she was sure Suzy Q didn't have a doll or that the little boy Timmy, who also lived at the Haveahordes, didn't have a car. The rest of that weekend Veronica spent trying to decide which of her many dolls she would choose to dress up and all the time thinking how she would laugh when Suzy would arrive with no doll and probably dressed in one of her cast off dresses, which her Mother always gave to the orphans.

Monday morning Mrs. Hobnob walked to school with Veronica and after telling Miss Twinkle-eyes what she wished to do, she told the room full of students. All the children clapped and cheered. Then Mrs. Hobnob left and the teacher put them to studying.

Lunchtime arrived and every one was so excited they never ate all their lunches. That is all but Suzy Q and Timmy, for the toys at the Haveahordes were pretty much a wreck from all the children that had played with them.

When school was out all the children ran home to tell about the party, all but Suzy Q. She was pretty sad, thinking about the dolls the other girls had and how she wished that just once she had one. Suzy Q didn't want to go home until she could smile and feel better because she knew Mrs. Haveahorde would notice her sadness and probably try to make her feel better by suggesting she make a rag doll or corn husk doll. She knew she couldn't handle her sympathy, without crying, so instead of going home she went to her very own secret place. No one else knew about her hiding place inside a grove of trees not far from the river. To get to it she had to crawl on her hands and knees through a wee tunnel of black berry vines and after going about twenty feet the tunnel opened up to a little grassy circle, like a room, with branches of trees over head that made sort of an umbrella. This was one time she didn't mind being so very small. The berry vines all around were covered with sharp stickers and the tunnel opening small. The other children had noticed the tunnel opening but Suzy Q had casually told them she just bet bears made the tunnel and she was pretty sure that would keep everyone else away from what she thought of as her Fairy Room.

CHAPTER FOUR

Suzy Q lay down on the grass in her secret place and started to cry, sobbing, "When is 'that day' coming, I guess it is only a silly dream."

As she started to drift into sleep she thought she heard a quiet voice say, "That day is here, please don't cry."

Suzy Q thought she must be dreaming, but opened her eyes and didn't see anyone as she slowly sat up.

"Over here," said the voice.

Suzy Q looked in the direction the voice was coming from but couldn't see anyone.

"Here, here", she heard the voice again, and looking toward the edge of the small clearing she saw what she thought was a bush and waving branch, but knowing there were only sticky berry bushes in that area she looked closer. As the bush started to move toward her she saw what she thought was a little child, under three feet tall, dressed all in green. The child had green slacks and jacket, green shoes and even green gloves. Suzy Q didn't know if it was a boy or girl because the hair seemed to be all pushed up under a green cap that looked like a huge leaf. This can't be real, thought Suzy, I have to get out of here! But, noticing her fear, the wee creature spoke.

"Please don't be afraid, I have been sent to help you. If you will tell me what Veronica has done now to hurt you, I will figure out what to do. I see you are afraid but after you tell me your problem I will tell you who I am and why I am here."

Suzy Q was so shaken and bewildered by now she had to sit down again. She had to find out who the wee one was, if she was real and why in a way it all seemed real, so she decided to tell her problems and see what happened next.

Suzy Q told about the party and that she had no doll and Timmy no car, and the wee one said, "Poof, that's easy to fix, so don't worry about it."

Suzy Q. jumped up saying "Easy, what can you a little child do? I can't believe you treat it like its nothing and Timmy will be heart broken with no car and Veronica will make fun of my clothes and now they also tease and make fun of my size because the other girls keep getting taller and I don't. Oh what is the use?" And she started to cry again.

Oh dear," said the wee one, "Please, please don't cry. I am sorry, I didn't mean to sound so unsympathetic but do sit down and listen to what I have to tell you and you will learn how I can help and also I think, why you don't grow much?"

After deciding things couldn't get worse and because Suzy Q had this wonderful imagination, she figured she might as well listen because after all magical things did happen and just maybe this was one. With this thought in mind she answered, the wee one. "Well, OK, I'll listen but I don't expect to hear anything to help".

When she sat down the wee one smiled and said, "I promise what I tell you will only make you happy."

Then the wee one started to tell a story.

"My name is Kestrel. My grandfather named me after a fearless bird he says lived in another land. My great grandmother was also named Kestrel and grandpa says I am fearless like her. Grandpa always had a story about everyone's name and its fun listening to him but instead of discussing grandpa I will tell you about our people. I am sure you have read about the little people in lots of different countries, like the Trolls in Norway; Leprechauns in Ireland and the fairies, gnome's elves and wee ones in other countries. My people and I are the wee folks of North America. We live all over America from Alaska to Panama. I've heard we even have distant relatives in South America but we don't know much about them. We have been here forever. My Grandpa who is two hundred years old says we were here before the Native Americans. He says we used to just call the different groups of us and other families Kin but when the huge people came from over the ocean and the Kin heard they named our land America, our Great grandpa growled and grumped about it for months. Then one day he said he had guessed it was all right because we had never had a name for our continent and now we would just call our different families and groups the Merry Kins. In fact he finally decided it was a great name because it would remind us to always be merry and helpful which was our role in life. He thought it too bad the giant people could not do the same. Of course Great-grandpa never said whether or not our role in life included our magic or the tricks we played on pompous giants. He always said it was just simple fun, as we never harmed anyone so why mention it. He also said he didn't like calling the huge people giants because they weren't true giants so he named them Toobigs. When more and more Toobigs arrived in America and started moving west, so did grandpa and his people. After he had traveled all over the area now called Washington and with the help of Aquila's father, he had found this beautiful little hidden valley on the Olympic Peninsula. He was sure his people would always be hidden and safe in this lovely haven so he named the village Hidden Hamlet. Of course the Kin shortened the name to The Ham."

At this point in her story Kestrel noticed Suzy Q looking at her oddly so she asked her, "Why the questioning look?"

Suzy Q answered. "Why should I believe a little child like you? What you are telling me must be a fairy tale your mother or father told you."

Kestrel realized that Suzy Q had reason to question the story when she thought about it from the way a giant person would look at her, so Kestrel decided she better explain about herself before continuing, so she said, "You are right Suzy Q. I should have told you about myself first so you could believe me. You will also learn who you are, who I am and why I am here."

For some reason Suzy Q now believed Kestrel and she just knew this was "The Day", the one that would change her life.

Kestrel went back to her story by saying that she was not a child but a twenty-two year old girl and she took off her green leaf hat and long dark brown hair tumbled about her shoulders.

She had lovely golden skin, the color Suzy Q's became from the summer sun. Without her hat she looked older.

The story continued with Kestrel telling of her and the Merry Kins home deep in the forest of the Olympic Mountains. She said she knew there were many, many things to explain about how they lived but as it would take a long time and it was getting late she would tell her the most important and then Suzy Q could go home and she would tell her more tomorrow.

Kestrel walked over to where Suzy Q was sitting and putting her arms around her gave her a hug and said, "The Merry Kins are your family, now go home and rest and tomorrow I will tell you your family story."

"Please, please tell me now" begged Suzy Q, "I have waited so long. I can't go home without knowing all, I'll never sleep, please tell me."

Kestrel would have liked to tell all now but it was getting late in the day and soon it would be dark. She finally convinced Suzy Q to go home by telling her that if she didn't people would come hunting for her and maybe learn her secret. Finally Suzy Q. agreed to wait until the next afternoon and then ran home.

Nobody at the Haveahorde's ever noticed a child was late as long as every chair had a child in it at meal time and the only job the youngest children, like Suzy Q had, was to clean off the table after dinner. Suzy Q arrived home just in time for dinner. After helping clean the table she did her homework and got ready for bed. It was hard to keep her mind on what she was doing as all she could think about was tomorrow and what she'd learn about family. Soon it was time for bed and Suzy Q was sure she couldn't sleep but the excitement had tired her and soon she was dozing off with her last thought before sleep, I have a family, yes! I never thought "That Day" I dreamed of would be so wonderful.

CHAPTER FIVE

The next day couldn't go fast enough for Suzy Q. Classes seemed hours long and even Miss Twinkle-eyes wandered why her favorite student was so fidgety. It was such a beautiful spring day after the long winter and no one was as happy about it as Suzy Q, for they were let out an hour early because of teacher's conference. Now Suzy Q knew she would have enough time for Kestrel's story. She walked slowly towards home, dawdling, so all the kids would get ahead of her and wouldn't see where she was going. When they finally were blocks ahead, she ran for her secret place and found Kestrel waiting for her.

Suzy Q just couldn't wait any longer. "Please tell me now, please, please, please," she begged.

"Do settle down and relax on the grass and I will finish the story," said Kestrel. "You are way too excited. Here have a drink of this cold water and calm yourself."

Suzy Q took a sip of water from the small bottle offered to her. It tasted different than just water, was a fleeting thought she had, but she quit shaking and became calm.

Kestrel started talking. "Yesterday I told you the Merry Kins were your family and it is true. When your mother was twelve years old she went berry picking alone which was usually safe enough, but alas not for your mother. We all knew there was an old hermit who lived deep in the forest but we all avoided his wanderings and never left a clue of our existence. We will never know how he spotted your mother but he did, and thinking she was a little lost child he took her to the house where you were found, because he knew a doctor lived there each summer. The doctor had a wife and twelve year old boy. His wife was very ill and he was just leaving for Seattle, where there were many hospitals

and doctors, and she could get better care then he could give. He
also thought their house in Seattle was better for her. He was in a
hurry and because he didn't recognize the child, your mother, or
believed the child belonged to any one in the town he took her
along. He expected to hear about a lost child on the news so he
could return her to her parents. Days and weeks went by and
though the good doctor inquired far and near there never was any
mention of a lost child. By this time the doctor's wife Susanna was
cured of her illness and wanted to keep the little girl. All this time
your mother had never spoken, thinking if she pretended to be
only two years old, like they thought she was, she could escape.
One day Susanna took your mother down town Seattle and when
your Mother saw all the cars, busses and trucks, even though she'd
read about them, she knew it was just too hazardous for one her
size to try to escape and find her way home."

Kestrel continued the story saying, "The day after the trip
down town Suzy Q's mother decided it was time to talk. She was
having breakfast and when Susanna handed her a glass of milk she
said, thank you. This so surprised Susanna that she dropped a
dish, the doctor just stared and their son Tory jumped up and
yelled, 'I knew it, I knew she could talk'.

"It took a while for the three Raldo's, for that was their name,
to realize what had just happened and then Dr. Raldo asked her if
she knew other words and what she could tell them about herself
and where she was from.

"Your mother than spoke saying of course she would tell as
much as she could. She said her name was Karinda Kin. She added
the Kin for she figured she needed two names to satisfy them.
Karinda said the hermit had stolen her because he thought she
was only a small child but she was really twelve years old. She said
all of her family were small like her and they would probably not
hunt for her, as they didn't want big people to know about them.
She also said she was sure they knew she was safe living with a
doctor, as they had ways of finding out the news, so for now they
wouldn't worry about her. Someday they were sure she'd return.
Karinda wouldn't know until years later that she was right about

her family knowing she was safe and where she was, she only knew it was possible and some day she'd know how they took care of her. When she finished talking, Tory sat enthralled. He believed every word she said. Dr. Raldo believed only part of her story. He was sure she could find her family if she wanted to but not knowing what to say just then he told Karinda they must seriously consider what to do. Dr. Raldo asked her if she would like them to take her back to the peninsula and they would hunt for the family if she didn't think her parents would search for her. Karinda said that just wouldn't help because after all they were on vacation and didn't live there but lived some where in Oregon or was it Idaho, she couldn't remember. After telling such wild lies she knew she sounded unreal but she couldn't have hundreds of people tramping all over the Olympic Peninsula looking for small people and scaring the Merry Kin.

"Dr. Raldo and Susanna saw that Karinda was getting distraught so they said they were very sorry about her being separated from her family and asked if she would like to make her home with them temporarily and wait to see if she heard from her family. This was just the answer Karinda wanted at this time for she was quite addled from the confrontation.

"That night Karinda couldn't sleep so she climbed out her bedroom window and walked around the garden for a while. She sat down to look at the stars before going back to bed and didn't realize she was directly under Dr. and Susannas's window until she heard them talking. Dr. Raldo was telling Susanna he had figured that Karinda was not truthful about some things. He thought she knew where her parents were but she was probably ashamed and embarrassed by their size or some other reason and didn't want to go back home. He said, he had been reading in a medical journal about causes for lack of growth in humans and talked to other doctors about it and they thought he should try different medicines they had heard of to see if it would help Karinda grow taller. He had told his associates about Karinda and said she was his adopted daughter. When it seemed they were through talking Karinda quietly rose and went back and climbed in her window. Poor

Karinda started to worry. What could she do if Dr. Raldo gave her
medicine and it did make her grow taller? She lay awake for hours
thinking and after a while thought she could help the Kin by
being a Big and on that thought she fell asleep."

Kestrel had talked so long without a pause she had to stop for
a minute to have a drink of water and Suzy Q took the pause to ask
the question, "What's a Big?"

Kestrel explained that there were a few, maybe one in a
hundred, Kin who for some reason grew taller than all the others,
sometimes almost four feet tall by the time they were adults.
Usually thirty-three inches was considered tall. The tallest ones
were called Bigs; and so named as a safeguard in recognizing
each other away from home. They were adult Kin who pretended
to be young boys or girls so they could enter the big people's
world. The Bigs sold baskets and other things the Merry Kins
made. They did the shopping for the Merry Kin in the Toobigs'
world and no one knew who they really were. They could move
about freely, with no need to hide like the rest of us, and help if
a Merry kin got in trouble. In fact there was a Big working as a
gardener for Dr. Raldo and watching over your mother, Karinda,
as soon as they could learn through their secret network where
she was. This secret network was made up of a few operators from
different Kin groups and only those few knew how it worked, so
that I can't explain.

After this explanation, Kestrel continued the story.

"Karinda was partly right when she told the Raldos her family
would probably not try to get her back at this time but of course
wrong when she said they wouldn't hunt for her, because of course
as I said they knew exactly where she was.

"The day after Karinda's disclosure, the Raldos asked more
questions and Karinda worried all day about her fate. She was
rather hopeful having heard Dr. Raldo call her his adopted
daughter. That night they asked her to come to the study. The
Doctor, Susanna and Tory told her they had been seriously
considering the situation and instead of just living with them
temporarily would she more or less consider it permanent so she

could start school with Tory next week. They told her to think about their idea and tell them on the morrow.

"Tory followed her when she left the study and started begging her to stay. 'Please, please,' he said, 'I always wanted a sister. I will take care of you and not let bigger kids tease you and oh just say yes, please, it will be to too too fantastic. You are so beautiful, everyone will love you.' Finally out of breath he had to stop.

"Karinda laughed and said 'I'll think about it.'

"Karinda already knew she would say yes because in her family twelve years old was considered quite adult and had some rights to choose what they should do as long as it was a wise decision by adult standards. She was sure this was wise as she would learn so many things in the big peoples schools and someday teach the Kin.

"The next day at breakfast she told the family yes. Everyone was happy and Tory was elated.

"Doctor and Susanna asked Karinda if she would please call them Uncle and Aunt for they wouldn't expect her to call them Mom or Dad. Karinda said she would like that very much, so it was settled.

"School was to start the following week, so much of the time was spent shopping for school clothes. What a surprise it was to the doctor and Susanna when for the first time in his life Tory was interested in shopping and then stopping in a nice restaurant for lunch. His manners had improved one hundred percent, helping Karinda anyway he could. Knowingly, Tory's parents smiled at each other and were wondering what other miracles their adopted daughter would work.

"Tory and Karinda started school together that September and all went well. The first few days there were remarks about Karinda's size but Tory would simply say it was a medical problem that was being taken care of. No one ever questioned it as after all Tory was a doctor's son and also who could possibly pick on such a nice friendly girl who was also beautiful.

"The years went by and soon it was high school graduation. Tory and Karinda had enjoyed happy school days and wonderful vacations with good friends. Dr. Raldo was pleased to see Karinda grow to a height of about four feet, believing she had grown due to the good diet he had provided. But Karinda wondered if she was really a Big. She believed the Raldos had forgotten all about her life before the hermit brought her to them, and though they were happy years, she often wondered about the Merry Kins and longed to see them.

"Now that school was over the big decision for Karinda was what to do next. Tory was going to the University to become a doctor. He kept pressing Karinda to go there too but her mind was only on going home and how she was going to get there. One day she was barely listening to Tory when she heard the word teacher. She asked him to repeat what he had said, which was that if she didn't know what she wanted why not become a teacher. Oh bless Tory was Karinda's thought for that was how to get home. Become a teacher and apply to teach on the Peninsula.

"The next four years did not go fast enough for Karinda. Both she and Tory spent hours studying with only an occasional outing. Finally she had her diploma and the first thing she did was apply for a teaching position on the Peninsula."

Kestrel now took another rest from her story telling and asked Suzy Q to guess where her mother taught.

Suzy Q didn't have to think about it at all for she seemed to know and with a thrill in her voice said, "The same school I go to".

Kestrel laughed happily and replied "Absolutely right!"

Then Kestrel continued, "When Karinda told her adopted family where she was going to teach they weren't a bit surprised for they realized she had always kept part of her early life secret and believed she was going back to find her family. They were happy for her as they realized she must have missed them all of these years. Doctor and Susanna hoped she found what she must have been looking for, as they were both getting old and were not too well. Tory felt very sad she was going, but he was so busy as an intern he didn't have any free time. They all promised to visit the following summer. She left for the peninsula a month before school started, which no one questioned. She said she must get settled in her new home."

Kestrel paused for a sip of water and then continued, "Karinda stepped off the bus at Forks and her only thought was home at last. She was all bewildered not knowing where to go or what to do first. She knew she couldn't just stand there for, as a stranger in such a small town people would soon be questioning her and offering help and she wouldn't know what to answer as she wasn't ready to explain why she had come to the area.

"The only idea that came to mind was to pick up her luggage and go into a café, and have something, until she could decide where to look for Kin. As she took her bags in hand a young boy stepped out of a beat up old truck and asked if he could help. Karinda was about to refuse when she really looked at the boy. Oh no, she thought, it just can't be, for before her stood the boy gardener who had worked at Dr. Raldo's over the years she lived there. As he reached for her luggage she was overwhelmed with emotion for she realized he was Kin, and a Big. She stumbled after him and got in the truck. After stowing the luggage he got in the truck and started out of town. By now Karinda was crying and saying how sorry she was for all the years she could have spoken to him if only she had known and she felt she should have known. The young man begged her not to cry telling her it was best she hadn't known he was there to watch over her and carry news of her to the Kin. For if she had known, she might have given them away. He then told her that his name was Narvik and he was there to take her home. After driving some distance on the main road he turned off on a trail like road, the entrance of which was hidden by small bushes and trees that Narvik held aside while he had Karinda drive the truck. Narvick drove on, winding around boulders and up and down gullies and eventually stopped before this huge and horrendous jumble of boulders. Karinda was finally home."

Kestrel now stopped telling her story and said, to Suzy Q, "I'm not going to tell you how or where the entrance was to your mother's home or how it looked inside or about the gardens for they are the very same today."

"But why, why? I do so much want to know everything about my mother," cried Suzy Q.

"Because some day soon you will see it and that will be ever so much better," replied Kestrel.

Kestrel had thought she could tell the story in a short time and Suzy Q had been so interested neither had noticed how dark it was getting until they looked up through the trees and discovered a dark cloud over head. The sunny spring day had turned to a dark rainy one. It often did this in the Olympics but when it did all the children were supposed to scoot for home. Some times it rained so hard that water running down the mountains caused streams to flood and on any warm day the children would be playing along a creek or fishing in it, so the rule for the young was when rain started, go home. Suzy Q didn't want to leave but knew she must. She hated leaving before she heard the whole story but Kestrel promised to be there the next day. Suzy Q worried about her, she was so small, but Kestrel assured her she would be fine.

Suzy Q spent the first part of the night listening to the rain and worrying about little Kestrel. Though she may be twenty-two years old she was so little. About one o'clock in the morning Suzy Q was still wide-awake so she quietly got out of bed and stood at the window. She was looking at the little cupola on top of their one story barn. It was a cozy little place about four feet square, reached by ladder, where old stuff was stored. While she was looking there was a flash of lightening and she saw Kestrel waving at her from the little window in the cupola! Suzy Q was so relieved of all worry she hurried back to bed. As she fell asleep she knew that from now on when Kestrel said all would be fine she would believe her and she would also believe that when she heard the rest of the story Kestral would have a grand plan for Veronica's party.

CHAPTER SIX

The next day was another sunny day and at school every one was talking about the party and hoping the sunny weather remained. All Suzy Q could think of was hearing more of her parents. After school it was again a run to her secret place. Kestrel was there and they talked about the storm and waving to each other and what a cozy place the cupola was. It was just a short chat, as Kestrel knew Suzy Q was anxious to hear more.

The two settled themselves comfortably and Kestrel continued the story of Suzy's mother. "Karinda's home coming was a wonderfully joyous time. All her friends and family came for a big celebration and to hear about things which Narvik and the Kin hadn't been privy to while she was at college and on vacations. He had been able to look in the windows and to tell the Kin of parties at the Raldos' and of her pretty clothes and had watched her learn to drive a car. So the Kin knew about somethings. Karinda spent three happy weeks at home and then she had to report to the little school where she was to teach.

"Karinda discovered she really enjoyed teaching and she had a little apartment, which was attached to the school. All went well, the students loved her and she spent part of her vacations with Kin and part in Seattle with the Raldos. It was quite easy to visit her family during this time for she had told everyone she just loved camping so she had bought an old truck and would go to the forest on weekends.

"The third year she was there was the year Tory became a doctor. She went to Seattle to celebrate the occasion with Tory and his parents. She had never realized how much she had missed Tory until she sat chatting with him at dinner that evening. Tory was eager to spend the summer on a long vacation before starting his medical practice. Karinda begged him to spend his summer on the Peninsula. Tory's parents thought it a great idea and reminded them of the little house they were living in when Karinda was brought to them. Tory agreed and said he'd see it was cleaned and repaired with new furniture, and then his parents could also visit. All thought this was a great idea.

"It was a wonderful summer for the two young people and one day while having a picnic at the beach they realized they loved each other and wanted to get married. This put Karinda in a serious quandary for she knew she must now tell Tory all about her family and she was afraid he would think her daffy. She finally started telling him about the Kin but was talking so fast he had to tell her to slow down. This she did and to her amazement he was not at all surprised for he said he had always known there was a mystery in her life and he didn't care what it was.

"They had two beautiful weddings, one with the Kin and one in Seattle. They were very happy and for the next years Tory was a very busy doctor and Karinda kept house in the former home of her Aunt and Uncle Raldo which had been given to them when the Raldos had retired to Spain. Narvik was of course their gardener.

"After being married for a few years Karinda and Tory's happiness was complete for they had a beautiful baby girl and they named her Susanna Isabel Amanda."

For a minute Suzy Q just sat stunned and then she realized what Kestrel had said and she screamed, "Me, me, the baby was me." and she hugged Kestrel as she laughed and cried.

Kestrel let her vent her feelings and then said she would finish the story, as now it wasn't very long, but warned Suzy Q it was also rather sad. Kestrel said she would now call Suzy Q, Susanna for the rest of her story, as it would be easier. Then she continued.

"When Susanna was six months old her mother, Karinda, did not feel as well as normal. The doctors could find no reason for her to feel weak. She had visited her home every summer, but now she asked Tory if she could go home and stay until she was well. Tory knew they needed a place with all conveniences for now they had a baby. He sent Narvik over to the small summer home in Mini

Creek to begin fixing and cleaning. It did not need too much work as they did spend every summer there and when they were gone several Kin would keep check on it.

"Tory took a leave of absence from the hospital and May first they left for the Peninsula. For Karinda her joy knew no bounds. Susanna thrived and all the attention she received from the Merry Kins kept her smiling and cooing. The Merry Kins came mostly at night so they need not worry about being seen but some times if you looked closely you could see one or two by a bush, watching Susanna as she lay on her blanket.

"When Susanna was eighteen months old Karinda became very weak. Tory wanted to take her back to Seattle to the hospital but Karinda asked to be taken to her home where she was born. Karinda lay in her childhood yard and played with Susanna. One afternoon she asked Tory to stay with her for she must tell him goodbye. She said their 'Old man and woman of the mountains', what some would call Shaman, had been to see her for they wanted to help. They examined her as the doctors had. They said how sorry they were for they couldn't help. Tory started to cry and blame himself for not being able to heal her, but Karinda smiled and asked him not to feel bad but think of the blessing of Susanna. She told him all she wanted was for him to help the Merry Kin in anyway a Toobig could and let Susanna know both his and her people.

"Then she said, 'Tory you know the Merry Kin believe like the native Indians, that a supreme being gives us a path to walk in life and how long the journey will be. He decides when to take us to his home where we will soar like the Eagles.' She kissed Tory and went to sleep.

"After Karinda was gone, Tory was very sad but wanted to follow Karinda's wishes. He decided to give everything in the little house to the Kin for they could use it all even if the beds, tables and chairs were high he would cut the legs off and rebuild things. He would move things at night and tell any Toobig asking questions that he was moving to Seattle. It was when he was moving the refrigerator a thought came to him. The Kin need electricity. I must go back to college and learn about wind and solar power. It had to be one or both, for they had to be undetectable in the forest. His only problem now was what to do with Susanna. The Merry Kin wanted to keep her but Dr. Tory had promised his wife that Susanna's first years would be spent with Toobigs. She had wanted this because she felt that if Susanna stayed small she would never learn about her father's way of life. Though he wanted to take her with him he thought it best not to for he would be busy with college courses and working as a doctor to earn money. Working long hours would put his daughter with caretakers for twelve to sixteen hours a day and he was afraid he might not find good help. He had thought about just asking the Haveahords to take care of her for a few years but he knew there would be lots of questions he couldn't answer. He was also afraid that if she didn't grow like most children, doctor friends would be giving him advice and he would have to explain why he didn't want it. Dr. Tory Raldo thought a long time about what to do and finally decided to leave her in the little house. He knew the Merry Kin would watch over her and feed her and make sure a Toobig found her quickly. He knew the Haveahordes, whom he liked, would soon be taking care of her. The Kin would always be near her and could steal her away or notify him if there was trouble.

"When he came back he would tell the Haveahordes he had been on a secret mission and he wanted Susanna kept safe. He wouldn't explain more than that for he felt studying to help the Kin was truly a secret mission. He would also tell them she had been secretly watched until she was safe with them. He knew when he came back for Susanna there would be many questions and he couldn't bear being thought heartless. He decided he would secretly send money to the Haveahordes.

"When he left Susanna at the house he whispered the same promise to her he had said to the Kin. 'I will be back as soon as I can. It may take four or five years but I'll be back.' Then he pinned the name on her blanket. Susanna Isabell Amanda Kinsraldo. The Kins added to the last name was to honor her mother and it would keep people from thinking of Dr. Raldo, as most people had just called both Tory and his dad Doc."

CHAPTER SEVEN

Another day was about to end. Suzy Q felt sad and happy. Sad knowing she'd never see her mother, but then a warm happy feeling knowing some day soon she would see her father. She wanted to ask dozens of questions but didn't know where to start. Karinda was as silent as Suzy Q, neither knowing what to say now, so Karinda suggested maybe Suzy Q should go home and think about all she had heard and tomorrow she could ask any questions she had and then she would be told what the party plans were.

The history and story about Suzy Q's family had been so long and exciting that Suzy Q had almost forgot about the party, in fact it didn't seem important any more, but when Karinda had promised she'd fix everything about the party it did seem some what important.

Suzy Q spent hours that night before she fell asleep thinking of all she had been told. The news of her mother was very sad but being she couldn't remember her and that she had always thought of herself as a motherless orphan she could handle the pain she felt. Karinda had said some day soon she would see where her mother lived so she had one request and one question for the next afternoon meeting.

Kestrel as always was waiting for Suzy Q. As Suzy Q sat down her first question was, "Do I have a lot of relatives and are you one?"

Kestrel answered, "Yes, many, your Grandma and Grandpa, uncles, aunts and cousins. I am your auntie, your mothers' youngest sister."

Suzy Q threw her arms around Kestrel and with a cry of pleasure exclaimed, "I knew you were special, I just knew it!"

At this remark Kestrel beamed with pleasure. They chatted about the Kin for a while and then Kestrel said they had better get started on party plans because tomorrow was Friday and she wouldn't be able to talk to her again until after the Saturday party and the plans would tell her why.

"Here are my plans,' said Kestrel, "please listen closely as I won't have time to repeat them as I have much to do. Narvik has been shopping for me. Tomorrow morning there will be a box on the Haveahorde's porch. I don't remember your birth date for sure but it's about now so on the box it will say Happy Birthday Susanna Kinsraldo. Do be surprised when you see it and get excited wondering who put it there. You must not let on you expected it. You'll know what to do with the contents. They are for the party. Now I must go back home and get several Kin ready for Saturday. You won't see them but they will be at the party helping all go well. I must hurry because if I don't see Narvik's truck in Mini Creek I will have to find Aquila to fly me there, and he is hard to find some times, and if you wonder who Aquila is he's our dear friend Eagle. Good bye now and I'll be here Sunday afternoon if you want to talk about the party or anything."

Without giving Suzy Q time to say a word, Kestrel vanished.

Kestrel's fast chatter about the birthday box, Kin helping but not being seen and then the remark about flying and a friendly eagle had Suzy Q's head in a spin. At dinner time Ma H worried Suzy Q was getting sick she was so quiet. So she sent her to bed early and Suzy Q didn't protest at all for by now her head was hurting.

CHAPTER EIGHT

Friday morning the first child out of the Haveahorde's house just happened to be Timmy. He saw the box propped up by the door and yelled, "Hey everyone look some one left a big pretty wrapped box."

Nobody rushed out as Timmy was always playing pranks. Though Suzy Q knew it was so, she didn't dare go out.

Then Timmy called again, "Somebody come, its too heavy for me and it says Happy Birthday Susanna or something like that."

Timmy didn't read too well, but now he was believed, so a boy called Jingles went to help.

Jingles said "It's a present for Susanna Kinsraldo."

Suzy Q became very excited and kept questioning who would send her a birthday present, while everyone, including Ma and Pa H gathered round saying, "Open it, open it, open it."

It was time to start for school but no one would leave before they saw what was in the box. Ma and Pa H didn't have the heart to send them off so Suzy Q opened the box to cries of Oh's, and Ah's as a beautiful doll was unwrapped. Under the doll was a pair of rose colored slacks, a beautiful rose sweater, a hair ribbon and new shoes that looked just perfect for Suzy Q. Beneath all this was another box and on it was written for your friend Timmy. Suzy was as surprised over this as Timmy. Upon opening the box Timmy found a new blue shirt, slacks and shoes, and a pretty red toy sports car just like he'd always hoped for. There was a note for him that said, for the party. All the children clapped and said they were just too, too happy for Timmy and Suzy Q. Then Ma and Pa H said they better scoot for school and the boys and girls decided no one should tell about the gifts, so old Veronica, as they called her, would really be surprised and get her comeuppance. All the kids at the Haveahordes knew how Veronica treated Suzy Q and some decided they would just happen to walk by or maybe escort Timmy and Suzy Q to the party the next day.

Friday evening when all the work was done Suzy Q and Timmy had shampoos and showers. The big boys checked Timmy's ears and fingernails, as he didn't always wash thoroughly. When they were satisfied they helped him try on his new clothes and Timmy was thrilled that they fit perfectly. In the meantime Suzy Q was going through the same inspection by the big girls and then she tried on her clothes and they were also a perfect fit. Soon it was bedtime but first each girl had a turn to hold the doll and each boy to inspect the red sports car. The doll of course opened and closed her eyes and said "ma ma," but the boys were more interested in the toy car for its many special features. The doors opened, the hood and trunk came up, the wheels turned and the head light came on when a switch on the dash was pushed. Timmy being a very generous boy said that as soon as the party was over each one could have a whole day to play with the car, even the girls if they wanted to. Suzy Q being just as generous had been wondering how to show her love and thanks and made the same promise to the girls about playing with her doll, but when she added even the boys if they wanted to, all the boys howled with laughter.

That is all but Timmy who quietly said, "I'd like to hold and rock her some time."

No one laughed at Timmy for they all knew he got lonesome and he was so small no one had much time for him.

Saturday morning dawned sunny and clear, a perfect party day.

Timmy was making a mad dash for the door when Jingles grabbed him by the tail of his shirt and said, "No way are you going out before the party for we all know if you do, we will have to start the scrubbing of Timmy all over again."

This upset Timmy, as he knew he couldn't stay in that long and do nothing. He was a wiggly kind of boy and every one at the Haveahordes finally decided, though it wasn't his turn, that this Saturday morning he could look at whatever kid shows he wanted.

A few months earlier an unknown donor had given them a big screen TV. Soon everyone knew that watching TV was the only thing that kept Timmy from wiggling.

Immediately after lunch Suzy Q and Timmy were dressed and ready for the party. Jingles and his friend Bender were going to walk with them for they just didn't trust any of old Veronica's pals if they happened to get a look at Timmy and Suzy Q. Jingles and Bender knew that Veronica bribed the few friends she had with special treats like movies and candy. They reached the Hobnob's with no trouble and the boys left Suzy Q and Timmy at the gate. Most of the children were already there, sitting on the porch.

Suzy Q's best friend Sissy spotted them first and shouted, "Look at Timmy and Suzy Q!"

When she got over her surprise she let out a shriek and dashed down the steps. Soon all the children had gathered round admiring their clothes and the doll and car. All that is but Veronica, who was furious and her mind was going at full speed as she was thinking up ways to overcome this disastrous surprise, for overcome it she would no matter what. No one, she vowed silently, especially not Suzy Q would outshine her.

The Hobnob's gardener brought folding chairs and set them on the lawn. When the children were all seated they were in for a big surprise for the Hobnobs had hired some clowns and jugglers to perform. After the clown's funny performance there was another surprise, a puppet show. The children loved the puppets and shrieked, yelled and clapped until their hands stung. Next Mrs. Hobnob announced the last activity before the ice cream and cake, the judging of the dolls and cars. She asked every one to line up and said one of the clowns would judge so everyone would feel it was fair. The prize was a wristwatch for the girl and one for the boy. She really didn't care what boy won and she was sure the girl would be Veronica, that's why she had the clown judge. Poor Mrs. Hobnob was in for a big surprise, as she hadn't bothered to look at any of the dolls, for after all who could afford a better one than Veronica's family.

The clown walked slowly down the line of boys and girls. He looked carefully at each doll and each car and then announced the winners by having them step forward. He had picked Suzy Q and Timmy, which most of the children thought he would, but Mrs. Hobnob was so shocked at her dear Veronica's losing she almost fainted and she had to sit down.

When Mrs. Hobnob was somewhat recovered she marched over to see the doll that had won. She sniffed and rudely asked, "Where did you get a doll like that?"

Suzy Q politely replied, "It was a birthday present Mrs. Hobnob."

Mrs. Hobnob started to storm off but then noticing the children staring at her she tried mightily to regain her composure and forcing a smile on her face she told the children to place their dolls and cars on their chairs and come in the house for refreshments. Suzy Q hated to leave her doll and Timmy's car out in the yard on a chair but as all the others did as told she knew she must. When she went in to the dining room she felt a little better as she remembered Kestrel saying several Kin would be there watching that all was well. She would have felt even better if she had known all but the oldest of the children from the Haveahordes were also there watching. They were hidden in a big clump of lilacs along one side of the yard. It had been a great place to hide as they had seen the entertainment and all that had gone on. Several other children, too old for the party, had also watched from hidden places. Mrs. Hobnob suspected this but pretended not to for she enjoyed hearing town folk comment on her generous children's parties. Most of the watching children left when the party went indoors for refreshments. The orphan group did not leave as they wanted to be sure Suzy Q and Timmy arrived home safely, so they stayed hidden. Because they stayed they had the most hilarious story to tell that night.

Veronica got the idea the minute she heard her mother tell everyone to leave his or her things outside. It would be so easy and she congratulated herself for her fast thinking and cleverness.

Just as the cake and ice cream were served Veronica asked to be excused. She jumped up exclaiming, "I must get some aspirin for my headache".

Instead of going up stairs, she sneaked out the door and ran to get Suzy Q's doll. Her plan was to take the doll and drop her in the irrigation ditch that ran along the side of the yard and behind the lilacs and had lots of squishy mud in it. When it was found she would be ready to say it must have been thrown there by some of the older boys who must have been watching. When she got to the chair and picked up the doll the orphan children thought she was going to take and hide it so they all were ready to follow if she started to get out of sight. To their surprise she was walking towards them and as one they knew, the ditch, but no one dared to move.

Veronica now held the doll with a hand under each of the doll's arms and was about to take a step forward to drop her in the ditch when the funniest thing happened.

In a high voice the doll said, "Just what do you think you are doing?" Then the doll kicked her in the stomach.

Veronica was shaken with fear and dropped the doll on the lawn. Then what looked like a green branch, to the watchers, swung against her legs and Veronica went head first in the soft mud. This made Veronica so angry she lost her fear and screaming and bawling she tried to get out of the ditch. The sides were so slippery she kept falling back in, and with each attempt she would yell louder. It was so funny the orphans couldn't keep from laughing. They laughed until they couldn't move. Veronica was yelling so loud everyone in the house heard her and they all came running. Mrs. Hobnob ran so fast she was first on the scene.

"Mommy, Mommy help me," Veronica cried. "Suzy Q's doll chased me and yelled at me and pushed me in the ditch, get me out, get me out now."

The gardener came forward and without being asked he pulled Veronica from the ditch. Mrs. Hobnob was astounded at what her daughter kept screaming, which was, "The doll did it, the doll did it, find the doll, find the doll" that she couldn't move or say a word. Every one was stunned for they thought Veronica was upstairs getting an aspirin.

Then everyone whispered, "What has she been up to now?"

Their remarks released the tension and looking at mud covered Veronica, and listening to her wild talk about Suzy Q's doll causing her to fall in the ditch, it all started an avalanche of laughter. It was all just too funny.

The laughter brought Mrs. Hobnob out of her state of shock and she reached out and slapped Veronica. This stopped every ones laughter as she said "Can't you see she is hysterical and doesn't know what she is saying?"

Veronica was really angry now. To think her mother had slapped her, some thing no one had ever done before, and to do it in front of all her classmates. She had to prove she was right. "Just bring me that darn doll and I'll show you she can talk and kick".

This was too funny and everyone started laughing again. Mrs. Hobnob was undone, she asked the children to please leave and took her daughter by the arm and dragged her in the house.

The guests picked up their dolls and cars and started for their homes. All the classmates agreed it was the best party ever and they bet Veronica had been up to no good when she fell in the ditch. They thought she had been pretty dumb though to blame her fall on a doll. They didn't think Veronica a fast thinker and at this they all started laughing all over again. As they went their separate ways they continued to giggle, even some of Veronica's pals. The children who had been in hiding also were laughing as they went home and the people of Mini Creek smiled and thought that the Hobnob's party must have been exceptional.

Back at the Hobnob's, Veronica was crying and carrying on and trying her best to convince her mother about what had happened. Her mother became so upset she called their family doctor and since he was an old friend, and he wasn't busy and couldn't understand, he drove out to the Hobnob's to try and discover the problem. He couldn't find anything wrong with Veronica. Knowing Veronica's tendency to exaggerate to get attention, he drew a conclusion he thought best not to say, especially when he heard Suzy Q had won a watch. The doctor told them he was certain that all the excitement and such sudden hot weather that day had probably made her feel faint and she had hallucinated. That was the best he could do, poor man, and then her mother added, "Oh, I'm sure that's it as she's so delicate."

The doctor slightly nodded. He knew her Veronica was stronger than most her age. Veronica still carried on and wanted to know what hallucination meant because her big worry was what her classmates would think when she returned to school. She knew she must have a reason for her behavior. The doctor gave her a sedative and as she went to sleep she was anticipating her story of hallucinating to all the kids.

CHAPTER NINE

That evening at the Haveahordes everyone was celebrating and having a grand time. Ma H had carefully been hording pennies and had enough to buy a treat of ice cream and she had baked a cake. She wanted everyone to enjoy the same treats as the party goers had. Suzy Q and Timmy said her cake was the very best.

After all tasks were done, everyone gathered in the living room. Jingles and Bender said they wished to reenact what they had seen, as Suzy Q and Timmy and the others who were not there could more appreciate what had happened. They wished to call their act "Veronica's Downfall". Jingles disappeared for a few minutes and while he was gone Bender made a little speech congratulating the winners and their willingness to let everyone wear the watches if someday they were in need of a watch. Jingles returned with an old yellow mop on his head and an old rag doll.

Peals of laughter rang out and one child said, "Hi Veronica," and all laughed harder.

Bender than set the stage saying the hall rug he laid on the floor was to represent the ditch and the chair the lilac bushes. He was to play two parts and they would know the parts by his actions. Then he crouched down by the chair.

Jingles came with the mop on his head, stepping along like his idea of a girl walking, then stopped by the rug "ditch" held up the rag doll and in a small voice said "What do you think your doing?" Then he shoved the dolls foot in his stomach, and he dropped the doll.

Bender hit him with a branch they'd put on the chair and Jingle fell in the ditch. As he screamed mud, mud and pretended he couldn't get up and when Bender was supposed to come to his rescue they both started laughing so hard, thinking about the real event, they just rolled around on the floor and the others joined in by falling down and screaming 'Mud, mud, Mommy help me, get me out, find the doll'. Mrs. H was tempted to say something but she knew most of them had been hurt at one time or another by Veronica so she decided to let them have their fun. However, she did wander about the part of the doll talking.

Suzy Q knew the Merry Kin had been the ones involved. She could hardly wait for the next day. If the Kin could make things happen like what went on today it would really be fun to live with them.

CHAPTER TEN

After church and then lunch on Sundays everyone at Ma and Pa H's could do whatever they wished in the afternoon. Suzy Q ran for her secret place. Timmy usually asked her to play with him but today he was having too much fun with his car and timing it's run down a small hill with his watch. Some of the older boys were enjoying the activity with him.

In the secret place Suzy Q's first question to Kestrel was, "How did you do it or what did you do to make my doll talk."

Kestrel laughed merrily and said, "So I did fool you. Though you are still very young, you are a Merry Kin and smart so I thought you must have guessed. What we did was have one of our boys and my little niece Winnie run over to your chair. Our boy grabbed your doll and my niece jumped up on your chair. I had dressed my niece exactly like your doll and her hair is almost the same color. They did this while everyone's eyes were on the children marching into the house."

"When Veronica thought she picked up my doll it was really your niece," exclaimed Suzy Q.

"Right, my dear, and when she was dropped she lay still until Veronica fell in the ditch and then rolled under a bush. While that was happening your doll was put back on your chair. Our boy had figured she'd try to take or harm your doll and if she didn't my niece was to whisper to you and explain when you picked her up and then we'd find a way to switch. We were just plain lucky about one thing and that was little Winnie thinking to roll out of site when we couldn't help her. For a six year old she's a winner. You'll see."

After this last remark, Suzy Q was eager to ask more questions and the first was. "When, when will I get to see her, for she must be my cousin if you are her aunt too? When will all I want happen?"

"When school is out for the summer. We have heard from your father and he will be here to claim you the first of June. He will take you to live in the house where you were found and in a few days he will tell people, who ask, that you have been sent to a summer camp but you really will be coming to The Ham."

Suzy Q was getting so excited that Kestrel got worried and told her to drink some of her special iced tea. The Grandmother had made it for Suzy Q for she feared too much excitement for a young girl might make her ill but she also knew she had to be told so she would be prepared to see her father. The tea was from a harmless herb and had a calming effect.

Suzy Q drank the tea and Kestrel told her she was excited as well for they would all have a grand time together. If Suzy Q wanted to she could go to school and study magic or ventriloquism or other specialties. It will be a wonderful summer, she continued, and come fall your father will decide if you stay with us or go back to Mini Creek School for another year. Then she said she had to leave and didn't think they'd see each other again until June.

As Kestrel was about to leave she turned and spoke again, "I didn't know if I should let you in on a mystery just yet but as we need help and you are one of us, maybe you can try to find out something we don't know yet. We had a note left in Narvik's truck saying, "Who is Timmy?" and now we think it may be from a Merry Kin from up north. He is quite small and we'd like to have him live with us, not with Toobigs if he is. Maybe he can remember something if you sort of question him, but don't seem curious. It will be your first assignment as a Merry Kin so it must not be known to anyone and especially not Timmy." She then kissed Suzy Q, whispered farewell and left.

At the dinner table at the H's the talk was still about the party. The big question was what the ones hiding in the lilac bush had heard.

Someone had talked but it couldn't be a doll. What or who was it. No one could come up with a solution though several had ideas that it must have been Veronica.

Suzy Q rather decided the issue with her explanation. She thought of it when they said it had to be Veronica. She said "You know I've heard Veronica talk to herself when she was angry." Several said they had heard her too.

"Well then," continued Suzy Q. "I bet she was saying something like, 'If they catch me someone will yell and ask what do you think you're doing,' and as you said she was running. Maybe she was only close enough for you to hear the last of it. And I suppose she was shaking my doll, because she was mad, so its foot swung and seemed to kick her."

"But what happened to your doll?" Bender asked, "How did it get back on the chair?"

"Well, I did see the gardener carrying some thing after he helped Veronica from the ditch," replied Suzy Q "and there was a little mud I wiped off my dolls hand."

Everyone agreed that had to be it for it sounded so right. Even Mrs. H was satisfied. Now the conversation was only on how funny it was and how would Veronica explain it all when Spring Vacation was over.

The day vacation was over the students all waited to see how Veronica acted. She came into the room with a flourish just as the bell rang. When everyone was seated she followed her mother's advice and asked Miss Twinkle-eyes if she could have a minute. She wished to explain how she had hallucinated. It was a very highly imagined account about her thinking she saw a doll on the stairs when she was going for an aspirin and thought the doll was threatening her with a ray gun, she paused to tell them this was called hallucinating of course, then went on that she was so scared she ran right into the ditch and thought she had felt being pushed. She said the doctor had explained hallucinating and that's what he said happened. Veronica pranced back to her chair as some of the older kids started to snicker but the teacher rapped for silence and immediately started classes.

Noon recess was a riot as all the kids had their say about Veronica's great imagination. Timmy told them about Suzy's explanation and the first graders said, "That old Veronica needn't think they were dumb enough to believe her even if they were only six, and that she sure was wacky."

They all seemed to just think of the party as old Veronica and her doings and just forgot about it expect for once in a while when some one would say "Hi Hallo" and giggled. The younger ones asked what Haloo meant and when told short for hallucinating they quickly joined in saying Haloo, thinking it too cool.

Suzy Q tried during this last month of school to learn something about Timmy but though she spent hours with him he never mentioned anything about time before coming to Ma and Pa Haveahordes. Soon school was out for the summer and Suzy Q had but two thoughts, which were, when will I see my Dad and when will I go to my mother's home.

The first day of June fell on a Sunday. Suzy Q asked Timmy if he'd like to go for a walk.

"Where to?" asked Timmy.

"Well, I thought maybe to the east end of town."

"Great replied", Timmy "When Jingles delivered the paper this morning he saw a big U-haul truck parked by that house that is out on the edge of town. Let's check it out."

This news was very exiting to Suzy Q for now she felt sure her Dad must be there. She went in and told Mrs. H where they were going and then she and Timmy started their walk. It didn't take long to get to the edge of Mini Creek, but the nearer they got the more excited Suzy Q became. She had been by the house many times before but until Kestrel had told her she had lived there as a baby and been found there it had been of no interest. Now every thing was changed and she didn't quite know how she felt.

"Oh, oh look," Timmy fairly shouted, "it's all fixed up."

Suzy Q hadn't had time to walk out here since Kestrel had come into her life and so the change was astonishing. The fence and gate were mended and painted and so was the house. The lawn was mowed and flowers planted and rose and lilac bushes trimmed. There were curtains at the windows, which were all clean, and shiny. Timmy opened the gate and ran up the old brick path but Suzy Q just stood by the gate and stared. To her it was a perfect picture of a home for a family.

A nice looking, medium tall Toobig came out the front door and asked Timmy if there was anything he wanted or did he just stop to say hello. As the man approached him and before he spoke, Timmy was a little worried but than he heard the soft voice and saw the kind face so he got over his fear.

"Hello sir," he said, "my name is Timmy and I guess we were just curious because Jingles told me he had seen a truck here when he delivered the papers, so me and my friend decided to come here and see what we could. We all live at Mr. And Mrs. H's, I mean the Haveahordes and that is my friend Suzy Q by the gate. I guess she was afraid to just walk in."

The man was of course Dr. Raldo. He looked toward Suzy Q and knew at once this was his daughter. She looked just like her mother. He walked slowly toward Suzy Q giving her time to maybe realize who he was, for he knew Kestrel had told her he was coming. Suzy Q just stood by the gate looking at the man, slowly a tear ran down her face, but when he got close and asked, "Susanna?," her tears turned to a big smile and she in turn questioned, "Dad?" Dr. Raldo knelt before Suzy Q then put his arms around her and hugged her so hard she just knew how much he loved her.

Poor Timmy he didn't know what to think, he had heard the words Susanna and Dad, but he just wasn't sure if it was what he thought. If it was then maybe there could be a miracle for him too and for just a second he had a flash of memory. He seemed to remember being wrapped in a blanket by a tiny lady. He decided it couldn't be as the lady seemed as small or smaller than Suzy Q so he just forgot about it.

The man held out his hand to Timmy and said, "Nice to meet you Timmy, I am Dr. Raldo, but you can call me Doc. I guess from what you heard you have guessed I'm Susanna's father. Let's all go in the house and talk about it."

He took them both by the hand and led them into the house. They had a minute to glimpse the living room, which had nice furniture and lamps, with rugs on the floors and pictures on the walls. He took them through into the kitchen and asked them to sit at the table. He figured it would be less formal, and homier and he could offer them cookies and milk to help them relax, for even though Suzy Q had expected him it must still be a shock and he could see it had certainly excited Timmy. They both said yes to cookies and milk and while Doc was getting the glasses, milk and cookies, Timmy could be still no longer. He was so happy for his friend he wanted to know everything—in fact Doc thought Timmy was acting older than a six year old or at least asking questions an older child would ask and for a moment he wondered if Timmy was Kin.

Doc placed the milk and cookies on the table and then sat down. He then told them, what Suzy Q already knew, that he had been on a mission since Suzy Q's mother had died and was now back to get Suzy Q and they were going to live together in this house. He said he had been about to leave for the Haveahordes when they had arrived at the house. Now they all had to go to the H's and he would explain everything to them and Susanna for that is what her Dad called her, and she could get her clothes and things and then come live with him if she wanted to. Of course she wanted to. They all got in his truck and he drove to Ma and Pa H's. When they arrived and Doc started explaining there was such a babble of questions, Mrs. H had to call for quiet, then she took Dr. Raldo into another room to talk while Suzy Q and Timmy told the others about Doc as best they could. When all seemed to be explained and Suzy Q had her things together some of the children looked real sad at Suzy Q's leaving but Doc told them to cheer up for they could visit Susanna any time, but not during the summer as they were leaving in two days on a vacation trip. He invited them all over for lunch on the morrow so they could say goodbye to Susanna before the trip. This pleased everyone and now they were all smiling. Suzy Q said she was leaving her doll for all to play with and as they thanked her someone said that her father should call her Suzy Q or they'd think he meant someone else. Dr. Raldo laughed and said he would try to remember.

The next day the Haveahordes and their children arrived for lunch at what they now called Doc's house. Doc and his helper, Narvik, had a wonderful picnic lunch for them, on a big table in the back yard and by each chair there was a name card and a gift wrapped in colorful paper and tied with ribbon. Even the Haveahordes each received a gift. Doc told them to open the gift whenever they wished. Of course they all wanted to open them immediately and upon seeing what they had received all of them exclaimed, "How did you know"? The children couldn't understand how Dr. Raldo knew what each of them wished for. Doc just laughed and said a fairy had told him—but Suzy Q was sure she knew. It had to be the Kin. Doc then said it was to thank all who had watched over Suzy Q and he knew how good the Haveahordes were and that he had watched over her until Jingles and Bender had taken her to them. He had already told the H's but he wanted the children to know and not think ill of him. In late afternoon they all left, hugging Suzy Q goodbye and saying see you in September. Timmy could not keep a tear from falling, for three months was such a very long time.

CHAPTER ELEVEN

Early the next morning Doc carried a sleepy Suzy Q to his truck, which was packed full, and he took off leaving Narvik to care for his house. It took Suzy Q a good hour to really wake up and by then she saw they were on a track or sort of road, deep in a forest where the truck could barely squeeze between the trees and climb over small rocks and branches. Her Dad asked her if she was hungry and when she nodded he gave her a banana and a pint of milk. He told her they had been traveling for a couple hours and it would take another hour because they had to drive so slowly. He then asked his daughter if there was anything she wished to talk about.

"Yes Daddy," Suzy Q said in a low voice, "Kestrel told me all about you and Mommy, but did you really have to leave me and didn't you miss me and want to see me?"

Doc was so shocked at what she had just said, that he immediately stopped the truck and took his daughter in his arms.

"Oh Suzy Q," he cried, "Of course I missed you, just something awful and I did want to see you, but in a way I did. How I saw you, I'll show you after I explain why I left you. All I thought of at that time was your future because I was sure someday you would live at The Ham. If you did live there, I wanted you to have all the things needed for a comfortable life. I believed electricity was the biggest thing I could give you and your mother's people. I knew this would take hours of study and that, plus being a doctor, would mean my days would be sixteen hours long. Also, the longer hours I worked would mean the sooner I could come back and claim you and spend all my time with you. It has taken me all this time to acquire all I needed in knowledge and equipment to do this. The boxes and all you see in the back of the truck are part of what I need to make solar and wind power. Now I will show you how I saw you."

Doc reached over and opened the glove compartment. He took out a large envelope from which he took many pictures. He handed them to Suzy Q and she was astounded. The pictures were all of her. They were of her in a stroller, in the park, in the Haveahordes yard playing, of her at school and many more, including her dressed up for Veronica's party. Her Dad then explained how he had given the Kin a small camera, when he left her, and they had kept him informed and sent him the pictures.

By now both Suzy Q and her Dad had tears in their eyes and her Dad said, "Maybe I was wrong to leave you and I'm sorry. Can you forgive me?"

Suzy Q hugged her dad and then replied, "Oh yes Daddy, for now I understand you did it for me and for mommy in a way."

Doc started the truck then and they drove on towards The Ham.

Suzy Q's thoughts', for the rest of the trip, were of a Magic Land, for that's how her mother's home appeared in her dreams. She was about to ask her Dad about Kestrel when he drove around a large boulder and toward a big old tangle of sticky vines. She was afraid he wouldn't stop in time and as if by magic the vines slid to the left and she saw an opening just big enough for the truck to go through. As they entered the tunnel she looked back and saw the vines sliding back into place. Her Dad put on his lights and drove another thirty feet or so and they entered a most beautiful place. Suzy Q kept thinking, this is where my mother lived. Then she saw all the small ones, the Kin, who must be her family and Suzy Q was overwhelmed. She just sat and stared. Her father seemed to know how she felt so he left her while he stepped out and spoke to those near him. After just sitting and looking for some time Suzy Q turned her head and said "Dad." Immediately he came and helped her from the truck.

He now announced to the great number assembled around them, "This one is Susanna, whom I promised to return to you— only now her friends call her Suzy Q."

Everyone cheered and clapped and as Suzy Q saw a small figure step from the crowd and start toward her she yelled, "Kestrel" and ran to her. As she gave her Aunt a big hug, here in her mother's village, she finally felt at home. Her Dad asked Kestrel to take Suzy Q to meet her grandparents who where waiting in their home. They didn't want this first meeting to be in a crowd of Kins. Her grandparents' home was small and built next to a larger house that, Kestrel told her, had been her mother and dads. They were waiting for her at the door of their house. When Suzy Q saw the two elderly Kin smiling and holding out their arms to her she was overwhelmed and started crying with joy. She almost felt like her mother was embracing her and she was completely happy. They laughed and talked and time flew by. Then her grandparents told their daughter Kestrel to show Suzy Q all of the little house and the room that would now be hers. It had been her mother's room. She loved her new bedroom especially as it contained may of her mother's old toys and books. After seeing all the rooms of the little house, they said goodbye.

Kestrel asked if she was ready to see the rest of the village now or did she want to stay with her father. Her Dad told her he had to unload the truck so this would be a good time and he would see her at lunch. Kestrel led Suzy Q to an opening under a large tree near the tunnel. There stood the prettiest little church she had ever seen. The door was a little higher than her head and inside it was like the church in Mini Creek only everything was smaller. Kestrel showed Suzy Q the whole little village. All was built under the trees and some used rocks and old wood and built close up to the mountain so they would be well hid from Toobigs. To Suzy Q it was truly amazing. Most buildings were the same size but chairs and beds were all different size. There was an open sunny meadow where they grew vegetables, planted here and there so they looked like wild plants and a lively brook where they fished and swam. The brook was fed by a mountain spring, from which they got their drinking water but it made the brook too cold for swimming or bathing except for a fast dip. Suzy Q asked why plant and buildings and things were hidden and Kestrel told her that sometimes planes flew over and they might see something and investigate and then they would have to move.

The next morning was the start of fun and classes for Suzy Q as she started to learn about the Kin. The first person she met was Kestrel who came to her grandparents' house to give her a suit of green clothes. Kestrel told her that a long time ago, some one had said, put on hidey clothes instead of green suits and the name caught on. After all the suits were worn so the Kin were not easily spotted among the forest greenery. Dressed in her new green hidey clothes Suzy Q went with Kestrel to meet others who were just starting classes. There was Fern, Bebe, Dawn, Chuck, Hoot, Merlin, Phin and Dodo. Suzy Q thought three girls and five boys.

Kestrel led them through the woods to a cleared space with over hanging tree branches that made it tent like. There were tree stumps to sit on and on a little platform a stool. They all sat down and in walked this little old man with a long beard.

The man climbed up on the stool, scowled and said, "You shall soon all become good ventriloquists. I demand it, for we are short of voice throwers. You will also learn to disappear, plus magic tricks. When you have learned all this I will see you again. Now Kestrel and Echo will try to teach you." Then the little old man climbed off the stool, and said, "Ja! Godt godt.," and he disappeared.

Dodo asked, "Where did he go and what does Ja Godt mean?"

Kestrel and Echo stepped upon the platform and explained he always said that and Ja meant yes and Godt they were told by Dr. Raldo meant good. Somewhere he had learned these two Norwegian words and seemed to enjoy saying them so much that he used them all the time. As for how he had disappeared, no one had ever found out.

Then Kestrel added, "At all times he will be called Ger Vanir or Professor Vanir. Please remember this and show him all due respect for he is very wise and very old".

Kestrel sat down and Echo the young man about Kestrel's age said he would try to explain to children how they could throw their voices. It was difficult to learn but he said with practice they'd get the hang of it. After an hour they had time to run and play. Dodo seemed to be the imp or mischief-maker of the group and was busy catching little garden snakes and slugs to annoy the girls with. Dodo had picked up the little professor's favorite words and every time he got close enough to put a snake on some ones shoulder he'd laughingly shout, "Ja, Godt! Godt! Godt."

After the play time Kestrel told them about the powers of concentration and that some who could focus completely were able to do magic things like move articles. She said not to worry about it if they couldn't because there were many who failed.

At noon they all went to lunch then rested an hour. After lunch they went back in the woods to a place where there were swings and hanging ropes made of vines. Kestrel had them play and swing on them as they wished for she said they must gain strength an adeptness at this for it was used in hiding or disappearing if in danger. Her last trial for the day was for them to see how well they could hide. Some did better than others but she found them all and by then it was time to clean up for dinner.

Each day was about the same, practicing and learning, but Saturday and Sundays were free for all Kin to do as they wished. Suzy Q spent some time on Sunday with her Dad but she knew he was real busy so she was mostly with Kestrel. On the first Saturday, after being there a week, Kestrel and Suzy Q were talking about her Dad's work, which was trying to build a wind generator so they would have electricity and then goodies like ice cream. When Suzy Q said ice cream it made her think of Timmy and the party and she mentioned she did miss him. Kestrel asked her if she'd learned anything of his early life.

Suzy Q replied, "Not a thing but he does mumble something over and over when he's asleep. It sounds like a strange language. Something like ganda wiffle biffle but it isn't clear."

Kestrel was shocked and excited. Could it have been "Iggy Wando Iffel Giffel, he was saying?"

That's it, that's it, now I remember."

"Come on" said Kestrel, "We must tell old Mrs. Dubar."

When she was told about Timmy she became very excited for she was sure it was her grandson, for only her son would know those words he had made up. He had been a very shy boy and that was his way of telling his mother "I love you" when other's were around.

He had left home to visit Kin in Vancouver Island Canada twelve years ago and she had never heard from him. As no one but her son ever used those words, he had made up, he would only say them to some one dear, like a son, of this she was sure. She had never told anyone what the old words meant until after he was gone for years and then she told Kestrel, after making her promise to keep it a secret for she was getting old and wanted some Kin to know.

By some miracle he had been sent back to his own Kin. It had to be the answer. Maybe Aquila had carried him but for some reason left him in the wrong place.

"I must see the boy, please Kestrel, help me," begged Mrs. Dubar.

Kestrel thought the first thing to do was seek Dr. Raldo's advice. As Grandma Dubar seemed too distraught to go anywhere Kestrel asked Suzy Q to run and get her Dad. This Suzy Q did and soon the four were planning what to do. Dr. Raldo said he planned on going to get some needed supplies on the morrow and he would stop by Mini Creek and ask the Haveahordes if Timmy could go with him and share the rest of Susanna's vacation trip as she was so lonesome and missed the H's. That was the only reason he could think of to return so soon and get Timmy, as he thought Mrs. Dubar was probably right. He figured he better stay over night at his house with Timmy so he could tell him all about the Kin and where they were going and who they believed him to be. If Timmy was Kin and ten or eleven years old, as Doc thought him to be, he would react differently than a five or six year old and maybe this would help discover who he was. He told Mrs. Dubar he would let her be the one to ask Timmy how he said I love you.

With plans made and the day over they retired to their houses.

Dr. Raldo left early the next morning and Kestrel came to stay with Suzy Q for the two or three days he was to be gone.

Suzy Q spent most of her time concentrating on voice throwing and disappearing. She was getting tired of Dodo and his "Ya godt godt" every time he bested a girl and was set on really putting him in his place before summer vacation was over. She kept hoping that the H's would let Timmy go with her Dad for then she would have an ally. Maybe between them they could think up something as good as what happened to Veronica.

The Kin children were like all children and were allowed their jokes and tricks for the elders thought it honed the skills they needed when around the Toobigs. That is they were allowed it as long as they didn't hurt anyone or humiliate them. If they did this they were punished. The elders preferred happenings like at Veronica's party for in that instance Veronica caused her own downfall by stealing the doll and to them that was the best lesson for a self centered jealous child or person. Suzy Q knew she had a lot of thinking to do if she were to pull a stunt like that on Dodo. He was getting close to going beyond the rules and doing his best to get Hoot to help him. She really had to figure something out soon and she bet if Timmy came, the boys wouldn't believe he would work with a girl. What Suzy Q really wished though was that Dodo would change. He was Kin and she didn't like to think of him being like Veronica.

CHAPTER TWELVE

Three days after her Dad left Suzy Q was sitting near the tunnel just hoping, when she heard the truck. As it came into view she was over come with joy when she saw Timmy. He seemed as awe struck as she had been when entering the clearing but then he saw Suzy Q and yelled her name. As soon as the truck stopped he slid out and ran to greet her. Doc came around the truck and swept Suzy Q off her feet with a big hug and kiss. No one had been told about Timmy yet, so the clearing was empty. Kestrel had told Suzy Q she could stay by the tunnel and watch for them and that's how she came to be there.

Timmy knew the first thing they were to do, before he met everyone, was to see Mrs. Dubar so Doc led the way to her house. Mrs. Dubar, or Granny as most Kin called her, was waiting on her porch. She took one look at Timmy and knew who he must be for he looked just like her son, but first she must ask him.

Mrs. Dubar said, "Hello Timmy, do you know how to say, I love you?"

Of all the things he expected Granny Dubar to say or ask this wasn't it. In fact it rather shocked him and he blurted out. "Iggy wando iffel giffel."

She had meant to surprise or shock him and it had worked, it had triggered his memory. He seemed to be the only one surprised by what he had said as the others there just stood and grinned at him. After a minute, Granny gave him a big hug and called him Grandson. Then Doc explained the odd question to Timmy. Kestrel had just stopped by to learn about Timmy and as now all the interested people were present he told them what else he had learned and what he was doing. He had questioned the Haveahordes about Timmy and learned he had been found in the back of an old pick up truck and had been with the H's for eight years. They thought him an infant when he arrived, maybe a year old, but they were worried because he didn't seem to grow like other children so they weren't sure of his age and that is why he wasn't schooled sooner. Doc told Granny and the others that when he heard this he figured Timmy was about eleven years old, judging by all he knew about Kin, and may have been two or three when he was found. This knowledge also made him sure Timmy was Kin and being so small he didn't think he should live with Toobigs any more but with Kin. So he had to figure out how to get him to the Kin with out anyone knowing where he went, so he asked if he could adopt him. The H's weren't sure what to do as the Mini Creek Welfare Ladies were in charge. Doc said he had played on their fear about Timmy's lack of growth and being a doctor he said he could take him to the best specialists and send him to special schools. The H's thought this to be the best for Timmy so they questioned the town lawyer and Welfare Ladies and all agreed. Papers were signed and now Doc had added a son to his family and a brother for Suzy Q. His idea was for Timmy to live with them while they were there and with Granny when they were back in Mini Creek. Everyone loved this idea.

What a joyous day for Granny, Timmy and Suzy Q. That night a special meeting was called at the church and Dr. Raldo announced that Granny Dubar's grandson had been located and was now a new member of the village.

At dinner, before the meeting, Suzy Q had whispered to Timmy "Don't tell anyone anything until I talk to you." So when the boys gathered round him asking questions and Dodo and Hoot promised they would show him the village on the morrow he didn't say much but that he was tired and would visit the next day.

That night before going to bed Doc gave them time to chat and catch up on news each had to tell. Timmy didn't have much, just about the H's and kids there. Veronica he'd heard was upset because she couldn't go away all summer like Suzy Q. Then it was Suzy Q's turn and she told Timmy about the school for ventriloquism, concentration and disappearing. It isn't like a real school though, she explained, but you'll see. Next she told him about Dodo and the snakes and about tricks being allowed to a certain extent but that Dodo was almost mean. She told all that had gone on since she arrived and being he would be almost two weeks behind the other beginners she would help him catch up. She told him she was trying to plan a good trick and she was so happy he was there. She had this idea she said that maybe Timmy should pretend to go along with the boys and not pay any attention to girls. That way maybe he could learn what Dodo and Hoot planned, for one of the girls had heard from her brother it was something big. Doc interrupted to say it was bedtime.

Suzy Q's last words were "I'm so happy to have you for a brother Timmy."

Timmy replied with "This is going to be fun, little sister, and we will out do Dodo."

As Suzy Q was going to sleep she had to chuckle over Timmy saying little sister as she was bigger though he was probably older. The next day when Timmy and Suzy Q started for the cleared space in the woods they were quickly joined, first by Fern and Bebe who wished to meet Timmy. Next Chuck, Dawn, Woody and Phin joined them. Dodo and Hoot came running up and gave Fern and Suzy Q, who were walking by Timmy, a big shove.

Dodo grabbed Timmy's arm and said "Come on, real boys don't walk with girls, that's sissy."

Timmy jerked free and turned to help Fern who had fallen.

After seeing she wasn't hurt Dodo said, "Ah come on she's not hurt, I know that hurting others is against the rules, but that was an accident."

Then he smirked and turned his back to the girls. Timmy now knew what Suzy Q tried to tell him the night before. He also thought they would really have to do some planning as Dodo was smarter than Veronica.

Timmy readily fitted into village life and his new friends quickly shortened his name to Tim, though older Kin continued calling him Timmy. He and Suzy Q spent lots of their evenings planning and practicing. Suzy Q's highest ambition was to move objects by concentration. Tim wanted to be best at everything and it was quite an upset when he bested Dodo, at the test of hiding or disappearing. He had only been there two weeks when Kestrel had located all but Tim at the close of the day.

She finally had to whistle, her sign of defeat, and as she did so Tim dropped in their midst from an over head branch and shouted, "iggy wando iffel giffel." It was to be his winning remark against "Ja, godt, godt," and in his mind it now meant I love winning!

Everyone laughed and clapped and asked what he said but he just replied it's "secret." Dodo didn't smile or clap for he blamed Kestrel who hadn't done a good job, as teacher, or of looking. He told Hoot she favored Tim because she was Suzy Q's aunt. Hoot didn't agree but he kept silent for he was afraid of Dodo's wrath and he knew that now Dodo would do anything within Kin law to beat Tim, for until that day he had considered him self the leader and no one was going to out do him. Poor Dodo, he was headed for trouble thought Hoot.

Kestrel couldn't figure out how Tim had evaded her. The green clothes they all wore were very good camouflage but she was very good at spotting an odd movement or different shade of green as some moved about, for they were allowed to move at will in the test. That was what these Kin were being trained for, to be unseen, for if she couldn't see them she knew the Toobigs never would. She had an idea how he'd done it and if she was right she knew he had a special friend and helper and someday she'd be told.

Tim had been there a week and Kestrel had been asked to bring him to Professor Vanir. No one was surprised at this for he hadn't seen Granny Dubar's grandson yet and though not many knew it, Tim's dad had been a favorite of Professor Vanir.

After Kestrel left, Professor Vanir led Tim behind his house and there perched on a stump was a large eagle.

Professor Vanir said, "Tim I want you to meet Aqiula."

Tim not sure what to do, but being in Kin land he wasn't too surprised so he politely said, "Hello Aquila" and the eagle nodded his head and fluttered his wings.

Professor Vanir told Tim to sit down and he'd tell him a story that had started twelve years ago, when Aquila had followed a dear friend, who was Kin, to Vancouver Island. His story was that, Aquila and his Kin friend had learned to converse as Professor Vanir and Aquila could. Aquila had stayed on the island as his friend had married Kin there. The Kin couple had a child and when he was three years old they decided to go back to their Olympic Mountain home. They had sneaked on board a ship and hid as they thought the ship was going to Port Angeles. An hour at sea they discovered it was headed for Alaska. They knew there were Kin in the far North but they didn't want to take the boy to that harsh land for it was September. Aquila had been following the ship and as he had been told they were going home he also saw the mistake that had been made. The ship had been delayed leaving until four in the afternoon so it was soon dark and all the passengers had left the deck. Aquila flew close to the rear of the ship and with his good eyesight saw his friend motion to him. He flew down and they all hid under deck chairs as they talked. His friend asked Aquila if he would carry their son to his old home. Aquila agreed. They put their son in a blanket and tied it so he couldn't possibly fall out and made a loop, which Aquila could grab with his claws. They told Aquila they would be back when they could and then bidding him goodbye they sent him with their son, "God Speed."

Aquila made good time flying and only rested once, high in a tree, before starting across the Strait of Juan de Fuca. He was almost to Mini Creek when some boys shot at him and hit his wing. He pretended to fall so they wouldn't shoot again and glided into the branches of a tall evergreen tree. He knew he couldn't go much further. He saw this old truck approaching Mini Creek and thinking it was Narvik he waited until it parked and was empty then he glided to it, left the boy and was just able to make it back to a close tree. It took three weeks for his wing to heal enough so he could fly on home. Aquila went to Granny Dubars but never saw her grandson. He hunted everywhere for him and not finding him he figured out he had put him in the wrong truck. This upset him so he stayed away and wouldn't talk.

Professor Vanir ended the story by saying, "Two days ago, Aquila's sister, who had taken his place helping Kin when he was gone, told him his old friends son was back. Aquila's heart was healed when he heard and came to me with his story. I can tell by your big smile Timmy that you've guessed this story is about you. I have also told your Granny, but we will tell no one else until your parents return, and I'm sure they will."

Tim was a very happy boy and so grateful to hear about his parents he asked, "Sir, why can't we tell others?"

Professor Vanir announced, "Only a very few can converse with Aquila and it must remain that way, so I can't tell Kin how I heard the story. I am sorry."

"Oh that's all right Sir, I know and that's all that matters but I do wish I could talk with Aquila."

"I am so glad to hear you say that Timmy as Aquila now wants to be your special friend as he was to your Dad and if you'll come over at night for an hour I will teach you to talk with Aquila. We must keep it a secret so tell Doc you are going to visit your Granny and I will explain the secret to her. I will let you know the time and what nights and now you may go home."

With a big smile and a hundred thanks Tim left.

Kestrel had guessed right. Tim had special friends.

CHAPTER THIRTEEN

Days seemed to fly by to the children and summer was half gone. Besides the training the youngsters had chores to do. They gathered fruit and berries and cared for the garden and each helped their parents at home. One day while Suzy Q was picking berries she saw a little fawn sleeping in the bushes, she went closer to pet it when she heard a soft voice that seemed to say, "Please don't hurt my baby."

She was very startled and thought she was imaging the voice but then it repeated, "Please let her sleep."

Now she didn't know what to think and was about to yell to another Kin when she saw close by a mother doe and now the voice seemed to come from her.

"No don't call anyone, only you are meant to hear me."

This was just too much for Suzy Q so she smiled at the deer then nodded and walked away. She had almost a full pail of berries so she started back to the village and stopped at Professor Vanir's house. The children had been told if they saw or heard any thing unusual they were always supposed to tell Professor Vanir first.

Professor Vanir was sitting on his porch enjoying the warm sun when Suzy Q arrived. She greeted him politely and then told him what had happened.

The little old man clapped his hands together and said, "Godt, godt you have been chosen and now we have two who can speak with animals. I am so glad it is you for it's best when two good friends can do this, for now you and Timmy will share the secret, for secret it must be. You see if everyone could talk to the animals, the animals would get confused with so many people asking favors or having emergencies. The Kin know that I talk to them but think I am the only one who can. Now I will tell Timmy to bring you with him when he visits me and you too shall learn the talk of the animals. Now Suzy Q, go home and tell no one."

In the weeks that followed Suzy Q and Timmy enjoyed the time spent with the Professor learning animal talk and the ways in which these creatures helped the Kin. Aquila caught salmon for the Kin and the deer let the Kin ride on their backs during the deep winter snow.

Professor Vanir decided he would test the children early this year, then he would be able to hike up the mountain to his retreat while the weather was still warm. Three fourths of summer school had passed so a big picnic was planned with each child showing what they had accomplished so far. All were so happy about this that they quite forgot about Dodo and whether he was still planning a trick. Of course he was planning, in fact he had spent so much time thinking about it he hadn't been doing much of anything else, so he had no new skills to show.

He found the girls were no longer afraid of snakes or bugs so he must think of something different. Usually the last thing they did after a picnic like this was a race across the meadow where a bucket of gifts was hung. A rope hung from it just out of reach of the tallest one but everyone had a chance to jump and reach it and tip it over so the goodies fell out for all to grab at. This bucket was to figure in his plan he decided, if he had to work all night. He hoped Suzy Q would be directly under it, for she was the tallest, and the one he was really aiming at. Suzy Q and Tim were his nemesis, his annoyers. He hated the fact Tim and Suzy Q were so well liked. The day of the picnic arrived and everyone had on their new green suits, all ready to have a good time.

Before lunch they were to have a magic and voice throwing show. Fern, Hoot and Suzy Q each showed their skill at moving an object. So far their skill was small, each making a utensil on the table move but they were highly praised as they were told how they would improve with practice. Bebe and Suzy Q each did a fair showing of ventriloquism. But all were greatly surprised because Phin, the quiet one, had carved a funny little figure that he sat on his knee and had tell funny jokes. He was so good at throwing his voice it seemed the figure was really talking. Merlin had not been able to be a ventriloquist but he had perfected imitating all the birds that dwelt in the Olympics. It was wonderful to listen to him and many birds were gathering in the trees above him to find the source of the calls. Professor Vanir congratulated them highly and told Dawn and Chuck not to worry about their ability for they may be needed as Bigs or special aides as that was why they had such a school to find each one's ability. As for Dodo he said he wasn't sure about him yet, he'd wait and see.

By now all were very hungry so they went to the picnic table and after Professor Vanir was served all enjoyed the feast.

Each helped clean and put things away after eating and then they rested for a time.

Next came the hiding but before they did Professor Vanir spoke a few words saying he had to leave so Kestrel and Echo would judge the rest. He then thanked all who had fixed the wonderful picnic and left with his, "Ja Godt."

After he left the children scattered and truly disappeared. They were getting very good at hiding. Kestrel and Echo spent an hour, which was their allotted time to look during the test, trying to find them. They had to blow the whistle and when it was seen no one had been found, this was the happiest group Kestrel and Echo had ever seen, for it was the first time everyone won. Kestrel and Echo praised them greatly.

It was with happy smiles they all lined up and waited for the word "go" to race across the meadow to the bucket. When the signal was given all ran as fast as they could. Hoot and Suzy Q arrived at the same time and jumped for the rope. The both grabbed it and tipped the bucket. Out poured wrapped sweets and small gifts. Dodo pretended to slip and then fall while running so he wouldn't be close when the bucket tipped and because of his fall and taking his time getting up he hadn't seen what came out of the bucket. He heard the screaming and laughter and to himself thought "Ja Godt it worked." He looked at the group but saw nothing amiss and by the time he got to the group all the goodies had been taken. He was so angry to discover that all his work and planning had failed and now they were laughing at his failure to get even one gift. What happened? It was supposed to be him laughing and enjoying his best trick ever. Hoot and the others, who had grabbed two or three things, asked him to choose one of theirs but he just shrugged and headed for home.

Dodo worried long into the night for he wondered who had known about what he had done and what would they do to him. For someone had to know in order to exchange the buckets. He had spent days collecting bits of grease and sticky black oil used on the truck and had mixed in cotton like fluff from different plants he had spent hours collecting. He had put all in a bucket like the other one and kept it in the sun so the grease would run. He had worked hard because without help he had to make a ladder and fix a pulley to haul the bucket over his head. It had taken half the night before the picnic. He had so wanted to see Suzy Q and maybe Timmy covered in the gooey mess. Exhausted from worry and last nights work he finally went to sleep.

Aquila was the answer to Dodo's wondering who had known what he did. Aquila had seen what Dodo was doing and had flown to Tim's house and tapped on his bedroom window with his beak. Aquila was very wise and thought it best if only one person knew and one who was big and strong so when Tim opened his window he said Tim should tell Dr. Raldo odd noises had been heard in the meadow and would the doctor check on it. On being told, Doc hurried to the meadow and was just in time to see Dodo remove the ladder and pulley. Doc had learned all about Kin tricks and stunts but he figured this must be something more since he was being asked to check it out. He waited some time after Dodo left and then placing a stump beneath the bucket he stepped up on it and looked in the bucket. Remembering Timmy and Suzy Q's discussion at dinner that night about the picnic and run for goodies he realized what Dodo meant to do and someone, besides himself, thought it a bad idea. He removed the bucket of oil and now he had to find the goodies. As he stepped off the stump he heard a distinct sound of stomping in a thicket. As he neared the thicket a deer walked out, seemed to nod and left. Doc looked where the deer had been and there was the bucket he wanted. He put it where it belonged and took the one with grease to the garage to hide. While he was doing all this he kept shaking his head and questioning what had happened. Timmy hears noises this far from the meadow, he gets there at the right time, a deer leads him to the bucket, so what next? Then he muttered to himself, "Just remember this is Kin land, anything can happen!"

CHAPTER FOURTEEN

Life went on as usual after the picnic. Once a week a Big would travel to Mini Creek to call on Narvik at Doc's house. He would find Narvik well and the little village quiet, which it usually was during the summer. There was nothing for Kin to do there or anyone to help and helping was their true vocation, helping in secret as Kin had always done. They helped humans and animals both but only the animals knew who they were. Older Kin would tell stories of helping Toobigs in snowstorms, of leaving food for hungry people and Christmas presents on doorsteps for Toobig's children when Toobigs had nothing to give, and many, many other helping deeds. Helping was the Kin's great enjoyment in life. Toobigs believed the good deeds had been done by kind neighbors, but could never discover who they were. One lost hunter said he was led to safety by an angel or a deer. People laughed at the hunter and said he must have imagined the deer as it had been snowing too hard to see. But all the Toobigs wondered to themselves if there were angels in the Olympics for no one had an answer. As for some of the funnier things that happened, like with Veronica, they just shrugged and said "Who Knows?"

On one trip Narvik told them the Fall Festival would be in September so they purchased the supplies that were needed and went home with the news. All Kin, young and old, spent hours making baskets, painting woodland scenes on wood slabs and carving animal figures for the festival. This was the only way they could make money to buy the wonderful things the Toobigs had brought with them to the Olympics. Many years ago, Bigs working for the Toobigs, when children were allowed to work, had discovered salt, flour and sugar in bags already to use. The Toobigs paid the Bigs with coin when the Bigs just meant to be helping. They swiftly learned the ways of the Toobigs and when returning home with flour, sugar and salt these Bigs told the Kin what they had learned and that the work they had done was easier than grinding grain for flour or hunting honey and getting stung by bees. Today the law did not allow young children, which adult Kin looked like, to work so they needed to earn money by making items they knew tourists at festivals would buy.

Dodo was doing his share at all tasks but everyone noticed he seemed to have lost all his impishness and wondered if he was ill. Hoot and the other children worried about him and were extra nice which he didn't even notice. He had so wanted to be a leader and now he realized he had been too much the wise guy and showoff and was sure to receive punishment that would cause him to even lose Hoot as a friend. Professor Vanir sent word for Dodo to come see him. This was the summons he had been dreading. He approached the Professor with fear in his heart. Professor Vanir asked him to sit with him on the porch and offered him a cold drink for he could see Dodo seemed nervous and almost afraid. The Professor wasn't sure why he was nervous but thought he may be able to help him by not dwelling on those things Dodo had not learned in the summer school.

Professor Vanir said, "Dodo, I hear you only did well in hiding but that's all right for I have discovered you are very good at mechanics. I would like you to report to Dr. Raldo for he needs help very badly with his work. If you like electrical and mechanical work, that may turn out to be your life's work. If not, tell me and I will try again to place you. This is why I said at the picnic for you to wait, I wanted it to be right for you. You may go to the Doc's at once."

Dodo was stunned on hearing this, after expecting punishment. All he could think to say was "Thank you Sir, Thank you."

As he left he heard the Professor say "Ja, Godt, Godt," and Dodo vowed he would never again use those words for they belonged to Professor Vanir.

Dodo was so puzzled. He wondered why the Professor thought he could be a mechanic and why no one had told him about the bucket trick. Someone must be helping. He would never know that Doc had visited Vanir and suggested he could use him as a helper for he had seen him making pulleys and such. Doc didn't say where, and Vanir didn't ask as he trusted him.

Dodo reported to Doc and told him what Professor Vanir had said. Doc pretended innocence in the matter and declared he was really happy to have help and hoped Dodo would like the work. Doc spent that afternoon explaining solar heat, wind generators and electricity to Dodo, using drawings and charts. He also told him he was planning on heating all homes with water piped from a hot springs near by. For the first time in his fourteen years Dodo was spell bound. He listened to every word and knew this was work he wanted to do. Doc saw Dodo's excitement and pleasure and was happy with the decision he had made. After the discussion, he invited Dodo home for dinner. Doc knew he was hesitating about the invitation because of Suzy Q and Tim but thought the best thing was to get any ill feelings over at once. Dodo finally agreed to come for dinner but said he must go home and tell his folks. Then he would be there.

Doc went home and told Suzy Q and Tim about the work that Professor Vanir had given Dodo and as they would be working together he had invited Dodo to dinner. When Dodo arrived he was very quiet, not his usual boisterous self, but Suzy Q and Tim greeted him as they would any of their friends and when they were at the table they chatted and joked until Dodo relaxed and joined in the conversation without thinking about past problems. Doc was happy to see this happen and after dinner urged Suzy Q and Tim to show Dodo their battery powered electronic games. The three spent a fun evening together and as the evening ended a friendly relationship was established that lasted for years.

Summer ended and the only sad note for all in the village was that Doc and Suzy Q must leave. Dodo had spent hours with Doc and was so good at following instructions and such a fast learner that Doc felt all his projects would be safe left in Dodo's hands and he would see him when he could get away. Tim, Kestrel and all the young said that if they had time they would come to Mini

Creek to visit. Suzy Q was glad she lived on the edge of town, where they could come and go secretly. Doc had worried about the Kin visiting so he told them he was going to fix up his garage storage room with all the comforts of home, including of course a refrigerator full of food, so if Suzy Q happened to have Toobigs visiting at the time of the Kin's arrival they would have a nice place to wait. He would put in a small secret door for them on the side next to the tree and he would have Narvik tell them how to enter. After all this was done he was sending Narvik home to stay. Narvik had given Doc years of help and it was time for him to enjoy his own village and family.

CHAPTER FIFTEEN

Doc and Suzy Q arrived home on a beautiful September morning. They had traveled at night so no Toobigs would know where they came from. By afternoon the Haveahordes were told of their arrival. Jingles had been watching for them, and the H's and all the children came to visit. They brought homemade bread and cookies and it was a great time. They asked about Timmy and were told he was doing great and in a special school. No one thought to ask where, though Doc and Suzy Q were just going to say back east if asked. They brought Suzy Q her doll but she said she wanted it to stay at the H's and then she gave them Timmy's red car, saying he wanted it to stay at the H's too. All were so pleased with this they told Doc they would all write Timmy if Doc would see he got the letters. Doc was more than happy to say yes. Doc asked Jingles if he wanted to work after school and weekends, when needed, as Narvik was going home. Jingles was pleased Doc had asked him for then he could pay for his own things like his friend Bender, who had a job at the garage. Both Jingles and Bender would graduate from high school the coming spring and they were trying to pay their own way. The visit was like all the times spent with the H's, a fun time, but now they said it was time to go.

School started on September fourth and the girls gathered around Suzy Q asking about her trip and about Timmy and saying how they missed her. Veronica tried to be friendly for her mother had told her she better. Now that Mrs. Hobnob had learned who Suzy Q's father was she must know more. The story she concocted from gossip here and there was that the H's were old friends of

Docs and as he had no relatives, he had left his daughter with them while he was in the Air force. No one knew how she put this together but no one questioned it or cared. To Mrs. Hobnob it was the two words, Doctor and Air Force that got her pressuring Veronica to be Suzy Q's friend for she was a snob and thus poor Veronica was being taught wrong values.

CHAPTER SIXTEEN

Suzy Q could hardly wait for the Fall Festival. She was up early and dashing about when her Dad came to the kitchen and commented on how late her girl friends from school had stayed to study. She said she knew it was late but if they got their work done on Friday night they would have Saturday and Sunday free for the festival. She asked why he had commented on it as he usually didn't, and did he think they worked too late.

Doc said, "No, but some might."

Suzy Q looked at her Dad's grin and yelled, "Oh, my gosh!" Then she ran outside heading for the garage. Why hadn't she thought of it she wondered, for she should have known they would come last night? She ran for the back of the garage and a small hidden door, knocked, and as Tim appeared she cried with joy. Sitting around a small table were four Kin and on the floor were all their items for sale. She hugged each in turn saying how sorry she had not greeted them last night. But they were happy when she told them she studied late so she would have lots of free time with them.

She wanted so badly to help them set up their booth and work with them but it seemed it would be impossible for every one in a small town, and especially Veronica and her mother, would question how she knew them.

"Let's go in the house and ask Dad," said Suzy Q. "He is good at solving problems."

Doc greeted them all and then Suzy Q told him their dilemma. He thought a while and said he believed he had a solution. He said he didn't think anyone should lie but that changing a location to help family shouldn't be called a lie. His idea was to say the young people whose parents had been his patients, which was true, had wanted to come to the festival and he had thought it a great idea so he was helping them and they were staying with him. If asked where they were from they were to say Seattle and that would be the location story. He just couldn't say location lie because maybe no one would ask.

They were to tell anyone who asked the truth, that the items for sale were made by them and their friends to earn money for special things. Now that it was settled, you couldn't find a happier group of Kin. All but Tim, for of course he had to stay behind, as all the Toobigs in Mini Creek would recognize him.

They loaded all the items for sale in the truck and as they prepared to leave asked how they had made a booth or table to display their things the year before. Cheri, one of the Bigs said they had paid a man several dollars for a board laid across cement blocks. Doc said that this year would be different. He repacked the boxes and found room in the truck for his picnic table and umbrella and a couple chairs. On the way to the park where the festival was held he stopped to get Jingles to help. Soon everything was arranged and Doc left after asking Jingles to keep an eye on things.

The first day went very well and the Kin sold half their goods. However, the next day was very different. Veronica and her Mother stopped by and bought a basket and some woodcarvings, as Veronica wanted to meet these new girls. As Mrs. Hobnob and Veronica were at the Kin's table several had gathered around to see what they were buying and quite a crowd formed. Suzy Q noticed a couple of scruffy looking thirteen or fourteen year old boys edging up to the table. As she was watching them the youngest took advantage of every ones interest in the Hobnobs and sneakily took a carving of a bear and put it in his pocket. He didn't rush off but put an innocent look on his face and stood in place. Suzy Q crossed her fingers and decided to try her new skill, 'ventriloquism'. if only she could do it. She tried but couldn't. She tried again and failed. Almost in tears she tried a third time and succeeded, for a voice came from the boys pocket saying. "Put me back, I can't breath in your pocket." Of course everyone thought some one in the crowd was pulling a joke and just looked around, then the voice spoke again, "You didn't pay for me so take me out of your scruffy green coat or I'll bite you." Now every one looked at the only one who had a green coat and he appeared terrified. He took the carving from his pocket threw it on the table, and ran before anyone could stop him. The Kin and Suzy Q had a terrible time to keep from laughing while the crowd was nervously trying to discover what happened. It took a long time for things to calm down, what with Veronica saying it was magic of some kind and how she had been right and not imagined a talking doll. Her mother kept trying to shush her and after getting her from the park other Mini Creek people just shrugged about it and said "Who knows?" If they had something special in Mini Creek they didn't want outsiders nosing around.

Tim was having a high old time. He wasn't about to stay home a second day so he was now perched high in a tree overlooking the Kin's table. His friend Aquila was with him and from where they were they could see everything. He had packed a lunch and been up there since daybreak.

The festival was getting ready to close and everyone was packing up. Only the workers who were selling things remained. The Kin and most of the other vendors had sold all their goods and had a good stash of money in their tills. Just then a dirty blue truck pulled up and stopped at the entrance to the park. Two scruffy men jumped out and headed for the vendors' tables. As they approached, they pulled guns from their pockets and yelled, "Don't move! Don't move!"

Frozen with fear the Kin and everyone else couldn't believe what they heard next. "Give us your money, now! Give us all your cash and do it fast. Put all your money on the tables!" As the men scooped up the money, all Suzy Q could think was, all this work for nothing.

There wasn't a chance to stop the men as they had over powered the sheriff and tied him up and they kept their guns pointed at the people as they went back to their truck. All would have been lost were it not for Aquila and Tim. They had seen the men over

power and tie up the sheriff just outside the park and Tim suspected
robbery, so staying in the shadow, on the far side of the tree, he
scooted down with the help of the rope he had taken with him for
that purpose. He told Aquila to follow the truck when it left. Tim
wasn't sure what he could do but he was going to try to help get
the money. He ran to where he had seen men building tables the
day before and found what he was hoping for. The men had left
any nails they dropped or bent laying on the ground. Tim picked
up all he could find and running to the truck he placed them in
front of and behind the tires hoping some would puncture the
tires. Then he climbed in the bed of the truck, covered himself
with some old sacks left there, and waited. Soon he heard the men
open the truck doors and start the motor. They backed up a few
feet then turned and sped off. Nothing happened for a quarter
mile or so and then the truck lurched sideways as a tire went flat
than another one went flat and they had to stop. The men were
furious, blaming each other for the tire trouble, as they grabbed
the gunnysack they had put the money in and started running
down a dirt road that led into the forest. They were sure they
could safely hide, but Tim and Aquila had other ideas. Tim followed
though with no hope of catching up to them unless Aquila could
stop them. Aquila dove at the largest man and with his great speed
and strong wings he knocked him over. The man never knew what
hit him and when the thin small man stopped to help him he
blamed him, saying he was trying to get the money for himself.
The thin man yelled at him and said it was an eagle. This was too
much for the other man and while they stood arguing Aquila had
time to fly high enough so he could once more dive at them. They
were standing so close and arguing so intensely that this time
Aquila knocked them both down and then jabbed the big mans
hand with his beak. The man dropped the sack and Aquila clutched
it with his talons and flew off. Tim had time, while the men stopped
and argued to get close enough to see what happened. He thought
it all just too funny. Here were two big bad robbers sitting in the
middle of a dirt road arguing about what they had seen or not seen
and so scared it was the work of some evil creature that they threw

their guns away, deep into the forest, and wondered where they could get an honest job. As they started walking Tim heard them vow they would never come back to the Olympic Peninsula and that worthless truck could stay here.

Tim headed back up the road wandering where Aquila was and how they were to return the money. As he approached the abandoned truck he saw the Sheriff, who had been freed, and some town people standing looking in the back of the truck. Then he heard the Sheriff shout, "Here's the money, I have the money!" He was standing in the back of the truck holding the sack of money. Tim couldn't understand at first and then he gave Aquila credit for being smarter then he, for dropping the money in the truck was the perfect answer for where to put it as the truck would be the first thing searched.

Tim stayed out of sight and by time he got back to the park the Sheriff had returned the money and after much rejoicing and questions most people left. It looked like he'd spend all night walking home but then he saw Suzy Q go back to get their lunch basket so he whispered her name as she past by the tree where he hid. She knew his voice at once. What could she do? Jingles must not see Tim, all she could think of was to whisper, "Wait, we'll be back."

As soon as Doc had let Jingles off at the H's, Suzy Q told him they had to go back to the Park for Tim. Doc started laughing and everyone wondered why. Suzy Q had felt he would be angry with Tim.

Doc said, "Well I'm not at all surprised Timmy is at the park and I bet he caused the stolen money to be in the truck."

Everyone had wondered what had happened to the robbers but Suzy Q and the Kin had never thought of Tim. The minute they got Tim safely in the truck he yelled, "Iggy Wondo iffil giffel." With that for a start they knew he'd have a funny story to tell the Kin.

To the Toobigs of Mini Creek it was another "Who knows" but some were a little shaken by the unexplained.

Monday morning all returned to normal. Suzy Q went to school. The Bigs did some shopping after which they spent the

day at Docs so he could take them home after dark. Upon arriving
back at The Ham the story was told of Tim saving the money and
of Suzy Q and the talking bear. All the Kin applauded loudly for
Tim and they intended to have a celebration for him and Suzy Q
whenever she came back. Dodo gave Tim much praise and told
Doc to greet Suzy Q for him. Dodo had certainly changed.

CHAPTER SEVENTEEN

Days passed and Mini Creek was again quiet and, as the kids said, a very dull place. Jingles spent time with Doc as an assistant. Now that Doc was in Mini Creek for the winter, Toobigs were coming to him with their health problems. They were happy they no longer had to drive twenty-five miles to see a doctor. Doc was happy to be busy so he fixed up an office on the main street. He taught Jingles how to sterilize instruments and give shots and many medical facts and things to do for the ill. Jingle confided to Doc he often wondered what to do after high school and now he knew he'd like to be a doctor. They talked whenever they were not busy and one day Doc asked Jingles where he got the name and was it a nickname. Jingles told him his real name was James Witmore. When he was not very old someone had given him the name and he thought maybe it was because he remembered asking his Dad over and over to sing the jingle jangle jingles song. Doc liked his nickname but told him when they were working together he would call him James. This pleased Jingles mightily. Doc asked about the other children at the Haveahordes and Jingles told him there was his friend Bender who wanted to be a lawyer and Maria who would like to be a nurse. That was all of the orphans. The other children were the Haveahordes and children in their care while parents were ill or working away from Mini Creek. All this was very interesting to Doc and he asked Jingles to dinner one night and for him to bring Bender and Maria. Doc was always doing the unexpected so no one was surprised at the invitation. After dinner he told his guests that Jingles and he had been talking about what Jingles would do after high school and Jingles had mentioned what each wished they could do. Doc told them about the big house his folks had left him in Seattle. He said if the three of them wished to go to the University of Washington he would pay their tuition and expenses and they could stay in the house. He had a couple as caretakers of the house so they only had to care for their own rooms and clothes. The three guests were in shock. Never had they expected such help. After the shock wore off they couldn't thank him enough, for this had been what they all wanted. Doc was pleased by their reaction and said he guessed he better know their real names as he had learned Jingle's name. Bender was using his last name, his full name was Joshua Bender and Maria was Maria Lightfoot.

When they were leaving Doc said, "Keep your grades up, for next September it will be the University.

Three very happy young people told the H's the wonderful news. Doc was happy they had accepted for he had an important reason. He was getting older and he hoped that one day he could pick one of these three to tell about the Kin, one he was sure he could trust with the secret, so Kin and Suzy Q especially his Suzy Q, would have a Toobig to help her, if necessary, when he was gone.

October arrived and the school children were looking forward to Halloween. Kestrel brought Tim to visit Suzy Q and she and Tim had dreamed up several ideas to surprise Mini Creek, but it seemed the little town was already in a state of wonder. The town's October meeting had been on the first and usually, as it was very dull, only a few people besides the Mayor and Sheriff ever attended. At this meeting the small town hall was packed full and most everyone had a story to tell and they never did have a town business meeting. Mr. Cotton who had a small farm asked to speak before the business meeting and started the story. He said he had gone out to his barn that morning to feed his pet goat and found his goat waiting for him with an old felt hat on and a scarf around his neck. These items Mr. Cotton always left in the barn in case it turned cold. His friends all had a good laugh, but the Walkers said they believed him. Mr. And Mrs. Walker, who were very old and frail, told of ordering a cord of wood, that the driver had dumped on their lawn. The next morning it was neatly stacked just where they wanted it. They wished to know who did it so they could thank them, but nobody knew. Then sweet white haired Granny Nelson, who had hurt her back, came to thank those who had picked her apples and put them in boxes. No one took credit. Dozens of like stories were told, but by far the best story was Mr. Jensen's. He had gone out to feed his dog Snoopy, who was named after the comic page Snoopy because one day he had found him sitting on top of his doghouse. Snoopy was wearing an aviator's helmet and goggles and around his neck was a world war one pilot's scarf. People looked at him and several said, "No way". Mr. Jensen said he figured no one would believe him so he had rushed in the house and grabbed his camera and got a picture of Snoopy. When everyone saw the picture they just roared with laughter because Snoopy looked so funny. After this the meeting broke up and now the stories were all believed and as usual people just shook their heads and said, "Who knows?" Granny Nelson said they should put a statue to "Who Knows" in the town square. Several agreed but no one could figure out what or who a statue should look like. At that all said good night and went home. The older folk wanted to end the discussion quickly as several had believed for years they had good fairies or some wee folk on the Olympic Peninsula. They didn't want it discussed at all for they were afraid people from far places would come and roam all over like they had when Big Foot was being looked for in the forest.

When Doc reached home and told Suzy Q they laughed and agreed they were pretty sure they knew the answer to "Who Knows".

CHAPTER EIGHTEEN

It was Friday. The next night was Halloween and all the school children were talking about their costume and trick or treating.

During lunch, Veronica and two of her girl friends and three rather rowdy boys were sitting together laughing and whispering. All Suzy Q heard, as she walked by them, was a name. It was old Purdy. After school Suzy Q hurried home as some of her Kin friends were arriving there that night and she wanted to be sure all was ready for them. Her Dad assured her he had put lots of goodies and pop and what he called junk food in their hidden room. Suzy Q was surprised when he said junk food, for that was usually a no no. She questioned the junk food and he replied, "Your right, I don't like junk food but remember the Kin only have it for special occasions so this is a treat for them."

Suzy Q put on her sad look or pout and asked, "How about me Dad? I don't get any very often."

Doc looked at her pretend pout, laughed, gave her a hug and answered, "Remember I said Kin. Does that not include you? Now run along, I think your guests are already here."

Suzy Q ran to the garage hoping to see those she had asked to come. Besides Tim she had asked if all her Kin Village classmates could come. She opened the door to the secret room and she was so happy to see them all there. Woody, Dodo, Hoot, Chuck, Dawn, Fern, Phin, Bebe and Tim. It was a very joyous reunion. Once they had quieted down they heard a knock. Suzy Q opened the door and her Dad came in. He said he knew he was interrupting the Halloween planning but as it probably was the only time he would see this group together, at least for some time, he would like to speak to them. He explained that he knew what he had to tell would be boring to them but he thought they should hear it. He had found a book of Kin history among his wife's personal things and in reading it had learned about different names the Kin gave to their children and why. Some of the same names had been used for years and because he had found the names of all present there he wanted to tell them. He commented first on Suzy Q and Tim's names, as they were not Kin names. Suzy Q had been named Susanna after his mother and the Toobigs had named Tim. It seemed they had picked Tim because he was so small. Years ago a very small man had lived with Toobigs and had been called Tiny Tim so they gave him the name. The first Kin name he explained was Bebe, short for Bluebell the lovely blue flowers that danced with the wind. Fern was a name taken from the plant, for ferns were adaptable to any climate and therefore considered dependable. The name Dawn heralded each day as being special, like a child was special.

The girls all liked what Doc told them and thanked him for telling them for they said they had often wondered about Kin names compared to Toobigs.

Doc continued what he had read saying, "Kin picked names sometimes from plants or animals they admired hoping the name would somehow help their child." He then continued with the boy's names, "Hoot was the name Kin called owls. As Owls depicted wisdom, Hoot's parents gave him the name of an owl. In this book it also said the owl made a low mournful quivering sound to a low hooting and Kin thought this a wonderful signaling sound. Each generation they named one boy Hoot, so they would know who was signaling. Merlin had the name of a hawk, a very swift bird. The name was also given to a great Wizard. Chuck was a name taken from the Wood Chuck, its real name being Marmot. Its great ability was hiding deep in the earth, if necessary. Phin was short for dolphin. A fast graceful swimmer and the dolphin seemed to have a special way of communicating with each other."

"Dodo's name," Doc said, "had two explanations. Dodo was really supposed to be Dode, short for Dodecanes Island in Greece. The name Dode represented the arts and the great knowledge passed on by the Greeks. Some time in the past, a Kin had written

Dodo instead of Dode. This mistake was only found about twenty years ago, the book said, when Professor Vanir had been reading old Kin history. The name Dodo was the name of a bird related to pigeons and doves. They were now extinct. They had lived on islands in the southern Indian Ocean. Our species the Bourbon dodo was a gorgeous creature with silvery plumage and brilliant yellow wings and tail. Its voice was a long wailing note. Because they couldn't fly, Dutch sailors called them dodoor, shortened to Dodo."

Doc summed up, "So that's a bit of Kin history. Hope you weren't too bored. Hope you all still like your names. Dodo can change his if he wants to. I talked to Professor Vanir and he said he can if he wishes."

Everyone looked at Dodo as he asked, "What do you think?"

They all agreed it was up to Dodo as they liked his name just fine. Until now he had never liked it, but after what Doc had told about his name, he decided it wasn't so bad after all. After a few minutes he said, "How about Dodo Dode, I like the original name too!"

All the Kin thought his idea was great and liked the sound of Dodo Dode. Hoot said, "Now all you have to do is develop a long wailing voice and we can both do signaling."

Tim sealed the new name with "Iggy wando iffil giffel."

All the Kin thanked him for telling them about their names, for they were truly grateful to learn Kin history. Doc said goodbye to everyone and left.

After he left Suzy Q said she had pretty well planned Halloween, if all agreed, but first they must tell her about their escapades and if the town people had told the stories about the goat and Snoopy and all else correctly. When she heard all was true she told them about the town suggesting a statue to "Who Knows" and this was so funny they decided they would have to come up with something. Suzy Q thought that the best idea ever.

Dodo Dode congratulated Suzy Q on her talking bear at the Fall Festival and this led them to the conclusion that they just must have a "Who Knows" Statue in the town center for next years

Fall Festival. Everyone must make a suggestion they agreed and maybe Phin with his wonderful carving ability could do a statue. They had lots of ideas after hearing about their names—like part plant, animal, bird and Kin! Suzy Q finally said she thought that should be left until some other time as they had Halloween to think of now.

Suzy Q said if anyone wanted a soda and some snacks, they should have them now while planning for the next night. Everyone agreed, so snacks and drinks were set out and when all were settled Suzy Q told what she had done and what she hoped they could do. She told them about hearing Mr. Purdy's name being mentioned at school so she figured Veronica and some others were going to make the evening very miserable for him. Suzy Q had gone to visit Mr. Purdy and thought he was a very nice old man, which of course the Kin already knew. They had been helping him ever since he had been alone. He had invited her in, inquired how her father the Doctor was and had offered her tea and cookies. He told her about knowing her grandfather, the old Doc. He thanked her for the visit and asked if there was anything he could do for her.

Suzy Q immediately said, "Oh yes Mr. Purdy and it wont be hard to do. Would you leave all your lights off on Halloween and not make any noise or come outside no matter what you hear? We, some friends and I, thought it would be fun to hide in your yard and scare anyone who would come around and want to upset someone who lives alone."

Mr. Purdy said of course he would do as she asked. He was a wise old man and understood what was going on for he had lived in Mini Creek all his life and knew all the "Who Knows" tales. He was like a kid looking forward to the evening.

Mr. Purdy lived in a very large old two-story house with porches all around and a turret on top with a catwalk around the turret. His yard was large, full of bushes, fruit trees and evergreens. He had a large garage that had once been a carriage house. Behind the house were a storage shed and an old barn. The yard and buildings were enclosed with a stone fence. His property was on a slight rise on the main street at the north end of town. It had so many places for hiding that the hooligans in the area had always made Halloween night miserable for Mr. Purdy. Suzy Q told the Kin she wanted to try and change this once and for all. Her friends were all for it.

Suzy Q gave her ideas and then asked for every ones help in improving them. The plan was finally set and all agreed with it. They were pretty sure Veronica and friends, whom they decided to call the enemy, would go over the wall in the back of the garden and start with the usual mean act of picking Mr. Purdy's prize apples and smashing them against the barn and house. When they started over the wall Hoot was to be in a tree and give the mournful sound of an owl, which he had been practicing.

Phin was to hide among the apple trees and using his ventriloquist skills, to say things like, don't you dare pick me, and ouch, ouch, now I'll hurt you, and whatever he could think of whenever the enemy reached for an apple. Merlin was to hide in the storage shed and if he couldn't find a good place where a flashlight wouldn't find him, he was to find a fast way out. Fern was to place herself in such a way as to look like part of the bushes by the shed window. When the enemy came near enough to her she was to rap on the window and Merlin would imitate every birdcall he knew. All were to wear their green clothes, hats and gloves so her hand on the window tapping would look like a branch. Suzy Q had wanted Dodo Dode to fix a ghost like figure, made from a sheet to hang in the big open door to the hay loft and have it sway or move but she hadn't known what to get but a rope. Dodo Dode found a pulley in Doc's garage that he said would do fine and he could have it in place within minutes of getting in the barn. He thought he would sneak in and look it over in the morning. Bebe was to hide in the lilac bushes by the front porch and if any enemy started up the stairs she was to use her ventriloquism and say whatever she thought of to scare them like "don't step on me". Dawn and Chuck were to hide in bushes on each side of the gates and make low moans as the enemy headed for the gate and out to the street. As Dawn and Chuck were Bigs they were to dress as Toobigs and follow the enemy into the town center and mingle with folks to hear what they would say. Suzy Q would try to follow the enemy around the yard and use her skill of voice throwing, if needed, to signal or protect any of the Kin. That left Tim and all he would say is he had to be at Mr. Purdy's by dusk and his action would be the big finale. No one asked about it for they knew he was being taught things by Professor Vanir and that Aquila was his friend so they were happy to be looking forward to a surprise ending. There were just two things to remember Tim told them. One was to be at the front of the house to see it, for it would come from above and two, every one was to be sure and moan, scream or wail as they moved toward the front of the yard so hopefully this would have the enemy heading for the gate to the street.

It was now getting late and everyone was getting tired so they decided they had better get to bed. Goodnights were said and Hoot and Chuck watched until Suzy Q was safely in the back door of her home. Then they went back into the secret room for a well-earned rest.

CHAPTER NINETEEN

It was a bright sunny day. All the Toobig children of Mini Creek were happy, especially the little one's, for if it rained they couldn't go trick or treating and would have what they called a dumb old party at home. There was excitement everywhere for even the adults were dressed in costumes. There wasn't much to do in such a small town so the adults wanted to make it special for the children.

It seemed everyone had their dinner early for by six-thirty the little ones were out trick or treating. Hoot, believed to be the fastest runner of the Kin was keeping lookout to see when Veronica and friends started out. Hoot watched her bid her Mother goodbye at eight-thirty and meet her Toobig friends who were waiting at her gate. When they started north on Main Street he took off on a run down through the alley to Mr. Purdy's. When he arrived he let all know he was there by a short hoot. The low mournful sound was the signal for the enemies' arrival.

It was a perfect night for Halloween. There was a big round moon in the sky but once in a while a small cloud scudded in front of it so it would be dark for a few minutes.

Fifteen minutes after Hoot arrived the Kin heard the low mournful cry.

Veronica whispered, "What was that?"

Back came an answer, "An owl dummy."

Then, "Don't call me a dummy."

The enemy was now all over the rock wall and heading for the apple trees. As one of the boys reached for an apple a cloud went across the moon and a voice said, "Don't you dare pick me."

Toobig said, "Quit talking and pick apples."

His friend said, "What do you mean quit talking, I never said a word." The third Toobig waited until the cloud passed then reached for a big ripe apple just as one of the girls did. This time a voice said, "Hey you two leave us alone or we'll bop you."

Now the six stopped for a moment to reconsider, but the oldest Toobig boy laughed and said, "No kids are going to play a joke on me, for that's what it is."

As he reached for another apple Phin hit him with one he had hidden in his pocket in case he got hungry.

This was enough for the other Toobigs and one said, "Lets get out of here."

They headed for the storage shed and Fern tapped on the window. Merlin started his bird songs. They were so clear and such perfect imitations the six Toobigs came to a complete stop to listen. It was hard to believe such warbling and singing at night.

One of the boys said, "Old Purdy must have a large aviary in that shed. If he does I bet it's illegal because I've never heard some of those birds before. Let's take a look so we can tell the Sheriff."

All six Toobigs started for the front of the shed, but when they got there they had to turn toward the door and were now facing the barn and there before there eyes floated a ghost.

Veronica and the two girls screamed and yelled, "Come on let's knock on Mr. Purdy's door, he's sure to let us in if we yell please."

As they were screaming and running for the front door Suzy Q managed to circle the house and throw the words, "Follow, follow" as a signal for all Kin to dash to the front yard. The Toobig girls got to the porch first and were up the steps and on it before the boys started up when all these voices seemed to come from the porch floor. By then Suzy Q and Phin had joined Bebe as the six were pounding on the door and yelling to be let in.

The porch was groaning and saying, "Quit stomping on me, ouch, ouch" and the door was answering with, "Don't pound so hard, your hurting me, please stop."

The Kin were laughing as they heard the Kin ventriloquists throw their voices. But the six Toobig enemies had turned and ran for the gate. As they scrambled through, they heard a swish and flapping of wings and felt something brush the tops of their heads.

Rushing on, they looked up and saw a huge dark shadow pass close over them. Tim with Aquila had been hiding on the catwalk and just as the six ran towards the gate, Aquila, holding a black silk scarf in his talons, flew over them and brushed their heads with the scarf. At the same time the Kin loudly moaned and groaned. The six fled in sheer terror toward the center of town. They screamed and yelled help so loud that the town's people and Sheriff heard them and came on the run. The Kin were laughing so hard they had trouble helping Tim down and retrieving Dodo Dode's ghost and pulley so they could all disappear. By the time the six Toobigs could manage to tell others what had happened, the Kin were gone and Mr. Purdy had a light on.

Shortly the Sheriff came knocking on Mr. Purdy's door and asked him if had seen or heard anything unusual to which Mr. Purdy replied, "No, no, not a thing."

When the Sheriff asked if he could look around the yard, Purdy answered, "Yes Sheriff, look anywhere you wish."

The Sheriff told him goodnight and as Mr. Purdy closed the door he smiled and thought yes, what a Good night.

When the Sheriff returned to the town center and reported everything was quiet at Mr. Purdy's, nothing out of place, no birds and no ghosts in the barns and furthermore Mr. Purdy had heard nothing, the six were furious. They knew what they had seen and heard. The older people just smiled and the young people figured the six had made it all up. That was the last time Mr. Purdy was ever bothered.

Suzy Q and Kin had a great party in the secret room as soon as they all got back to Doc's from their outing. The laughter and talk probably would have gone on all night but Doc came out at eleven to get Suzy Q as the Kin were leaving early in the morning. They hugged Suzy Q goodbye and they all promised to have Christmas together.

When Suzy Q went to bed she was extremely tired but very happy. She had really had a most wonderful night. As she was drifting off to sleep she thought, this time next year I will not be living here for I will be moving to the Kin's village, The Ham. She had not grown at all for three years and her Dad thought now was the time she should move to her peoples' village. He was sure as small as she was, she would never be happy in the Toobig's world. I can hardly wait, so much to look forward to. I wonder if I will like the Kin's school. I wonder if Tim's Mom and Dad will get home by then. I wonder if we can make a "Who Knows" Statue. I wonder, but she fell asleep in the middle of wondering.

CHAPTER TWENTY

June first and Suzy Q had arrived to start her life with the Kin and to live with her grandparents in her Mother's old room! Suzy had brought some of her things here when she spent part of Christmas vacation at The Ham. Now all her possessions were in her room. She had been so eager to move here, but now it was a little scary to think she could never again live in Mini Creek. She had not grown taller in over three years and her Dad thought now was the time to move to her peoples' village. He was sure, as small as she was, she would never be happy in the Toobigs' world. He could see that though she wanted this move it was troubling her. Doc told her to think of the fun she could have because she could dress as a little girl and he could take her and Kestrel, or a friend, also dressed thus, any where in the world or to think of the pranks and the good she could do secretly for Toobigs. These ideas lifted her spirits and she decided that being Kin with a Toobig father was the greatest.

Suzy Q had been in the village two weeks and had spent time fixing her small room just the way she wanted it. Her father had made furniture just for her. She loved her small bed with the blue net canopy and small fluffy pillows. She spent lots of time in her little rocker while deciding where to put her mother's pictures and trinkets. When not working on her room she spent time visiting and really getting to know the village and all the people. She spent hours with her grandparents as they told her stories of the past and about her mother as a baby and how much they missed her, especially while she had lived with the Raldos. She visited her aunts and cousins and had great fun with Winnie, the tiny cousin who had pretended to be her doll. She also liked visiting with Timmy's grandmother, Granny Dubar, even though it made her feel sad, thinking of how Granny Dubar must wonder about her missing son Bern. One afternoon while Suzy Q was enjoying her little room her Dad called her.

Dr. Raldo was in the kitchen preparing a snack for the two of them when Suzy Q answered his call. He was smiling broadly and Suzy Q decided her Dad must be planning something good or fun. Dr. Raldo placed the snack on the table and they both sat down to eat.

He wanted to tell her his plans at once, but waited until they finished their lunch. He knew Suzy Q would get too excited to finish eating. They were finishing the food when Dr. Raldo said he had decided on a trip and intended to take Dodo, Kestrel, Timmy and Suzy Q with him. Before he could say more, Suzy Q let out a whoop and asked,

"When? Where?"

He told her, "Calm down" and then he explained.

He said he had over heard Timmy talking to his friend Aquila, the eagle. Timmy had told Aquila how he wished he could go looking for his parents. Doc told Suzy Q that hearing Timmy sound so sad also made him want to find Timmy's parents. He had booked passage on an ocean liner, a really big and fun ship, and they were all going to Alaska. He wanted to try to find where Timmy's folks had left the ship after leaving Vancouver, Canada. He had learned the first stop the ship made was at Juneau, Alaska so that was where they would start hunting. He told Suzy Q they would leave in ten days so they had lots of planning to do. They must first sew or buy clothes, that looked like they were for toddlers, for Timmy and Kestrel to wear on the trip. The two must also bring warm sturdy clothes for they may have to go into the Alaska Wilderness. Clothes for Dodo and Suzy Q would be easy to get but Doc wanted to be ready for any adventure. Doc said he had already told Kestrel and Dodo so they could get started on all the arrangements. He told Suzy Q she could now tell Timmy and then Timmy could tell his Granny.

Suzy Q hugged and kissed her Dad and started to run off to tell Timmy. She stopped, turned back and said in a very grown up way, "Father I have a request to make. Now that I am almost an adult and going out among Toobigs would you please drop the Q from my name or call me Susanna? You know I hardly ever ask questions any more."

Her Dad, suppressing a smile replied, "Yes, I think Suzy without the Q would be fine, more grown up, but Susanna may be harder for your friends to change to. I leave it up to you to tell them to omit the Q."

Suzy rushed to find Timmy and tell him the news. Timmy then ran to his Granny's house and upon hearing the news she immediately started making the right clothes for Timmy. Meanwhile Suzy was telling one and all, no more Q!

The next ten days in the The Ham were a whirlwind of activity. Everyone wanted to help and contribute to this journey. Finally, it was the last evening, before their journey started. Everyone in the village gathered at town center for a happy farewell dinner. Goodbyes were said and around midnight the travelers climbed in Doc's truck and left for Seattle.

CHAPTER TWENTY-ONE

Their ship would leave in the morning, but Doc had arranged for them to board the ship in the middle of the night. By traveling at night there would be no chance of anyone seeing them. After Narvik, who had gone along, helped them aboard, he took the truck to Doc's Seattle home, where Doc told him to stay until they returned.

Doc had reserved two cabins side by side, each with a balcony. The four youngsters were overwhelmed with the wonder of it all. Though they had seen pictures of the ship and the Seattle waterfront, and lived among giant trees and mountains, and been to the beach, they weren't prepared for the immense size of the ship. Perhaps they were too used to their little houses and little canoes.

Doc hurried them to their cabins and told them they must stay in them until they had left port. He did say they could sit on the balcony but thought they should get some sleep first. Suzy and Kestrel were too excited to sleep after putting on their pajamas so they checked everything in their cabin, and then found a wastepaper basket Kestrel could use for climbing into the bed. They watched a T.V. program and finally felt calmed down enough to sleep.

Suzy and Kestrel had one cabin while Doc, Timmy and Dodo shared a cabin just next door. After Doc and the boys had prepared for bed and lights were dimmed Timmy decided to step out on the balcony. He closed the drapes and turned to look at the water and the Seattle skyline. He really wasn't surprised but he was very, very happy to see his dear friend Aquila perched on the balcony rail. Aquila made known that he was going to follow the ship and always be near in case they needed help. The eagle then flew away.

Timmy missed his Granny so much but having his friend near comforted him and he climbed into the great big bed and fell swiftly to sleep.

Doc and the Kin slept late the next morning and were awakened by the ships farewell horn. They all grabbed a robe and rushed out on the balcony to see what the noise was and realized the ship was moving away from the shore and they were on their way to Alaska. They stood on their balcony and watched as the Seattle skyline gradually looked smaller the further the ship went. It was very exciting to the children.

The first day Doc called and ordered meals to be brought to their cabin. They were sitting together eating on the balcony when they saw a pod of Orca whales. The whales were leaping and diving and seemed to be having a wonderful time. Though passengers had been told they might see Orcas in Puget Sound waters the sighting created much excitement and when Timmy looked down to the promenade deck he could see the Toobigs rushing around. Oh how he wished there was a way he could get close to the water. He just knew if he could talk to the Orcas they would let him ride on their backs. Timmy spent the day watching the Orcas and daydreaming. Toward evening the ship entered the Straits of Juan de Fuca, which led to the ocean, and Timmy realized his hopes for a whale ride were gone.

The second day was sunny and clear and Doc told the four Kin to get dressed in appropriate clothes for their ages. Dodo and Suzy donned jeans and pretty tee shirts and were pleased that they could pass for any young age.

Timmy and Kestrel had bib overalls and shirts size two. Timmy didn't mind wearing baby clothes for to him it was all about finding his parents and seeing that which perhaps his parents had seen. Kestrel was mortified for she was a twenty-two year old adult and now looked like a two year old. Doc could see her discomfort so he suggested she just think of herself as a great actress and to have fun as she did when she engaged in the Kin pranks as a child. On this thought they left their cabins for the first time to explore the huge ship.

Kestrel and Timmy, of course, had to hold Docs' hand as toddlers would. Doc had been teasing his twenty-two year old sister-in-law Kestrel, saying she better be good or he would ground her! They toured the ship seeing every inch open to passengers. All went well until Doc decided to stop on the top deck where there was a buffet lunch being served. Everyone decided what they wanted and Doc and Dodo carried Timmy and Kestrel's trays. When they found an empty table there was a rush by several women to help them be seated. They had seen this good-looking man with his children on deck and now they wanted to meet him. They oohed and aahed over the cute little boy and girl, asking if they could help by picking them up or holding them or perhaps feeding them? Dodo and Suzy Q got the giggles over the idea of their being fed and Dodo seemed totally helpless. Kestrel could think of nothing to do and kept saying no, no over and over. All of a sudden a tall husky woman reached over and picked Timmy up and hugged him to her. Timmy was mortified. Looking around he saw a suit of decorative armor and in desperation used his ventriloquist voice and out of the mouth of the helmet came these words.

"Ladies, ladies thin and tall
Have you no manners,
None at all?
If this man had wanted aid
He would have hired
A kind young maid
So leave them now
Be gone I say
And let this family
Enjoy the day."

When the voice started, the room became totally quiet and the women around Doc's table seemed shocked. When the voice stopped, the Toobigs, who heard what was said, laughed and clapped loudly. The big Toobig holding Timmy, turned bright red, thrust Timmy back into his chair, and ran from the dining room. The other women fled with her, leaving their lunches unfinished. The Toobig diners wondered what had made the armor say the clever poem.

No one imagined it could be one of those tiny children with the handsome man, but of course Doc knew. The four Kin were now settled, but it was hard not to laugh at what Timmy had done. Poor Doc. He knew he had to scold Timmy for embarrassing the women, but how, he wondered, when he was secretly glad to be rid of the women.

When lunch was over they started back to their cabin. Timmy worried all the way for he knew he was not supposed to hurt any ones feelings. He wandered what his punishment would be and since he was so worried he started talking as soon as they were in the cabin and the door was closed.

"Doc I'm so sorry, but I could see Kestrel was upset, imagine them wanting to hold and feed a teenage boy and a twenty-two year old woman even if they didn't know how old we were, they were strangers and they should have left us alone and I didn't think about it embarrassing the ladies I just wanted them to go away cause at my age I was embarrassed too and I had to do something in a hurry and I know my poetry was awful but I didn't have time to say it right and I am sorry and . . ."

Doc yelled, "Timmy stop, I am not going to scold you and after hearing what you said and remembering how I felt at your age, we will say no more about it. Also, I know the circumstances were unusual and you spoke in haste, for I know you wouldn't deliberately embarrass the ladies."

Then turning away from Timmy he winked and grinned at the others and said, "Your poetry was pretty bad, but at least it rhymed."

That night they were going to the fancy dining room so they dressed in their finest clothes for it was dress up night. Kestrel was really excited because she had often read about such affairs but never dreamed of being at one. The three guys seemed unconcerned about it all. Doc, Dodo and even Timmy had a Tuxedo with red cummerbunds. Suzy and Kestrel had long silk dresses and Kestrel looked, to the Toobigs, like a beautiful doll. When they reached the dining room all eyes turned their way for it seemed everyone aboard ship had heard what happened at lunch and now to see them looking so elegant, when they were expecting to see four little kids, seemed unbelievable. Doc had planned ahead and ordered two chairs that looked like all the others, but had longer legs so the seats were higher for Timmy and Kestrel. There also was an extra rung for them to step on and reach the seat and with Doc and the waiters' help they were all smoothly seated.

The waiter started to pass menus, skipping Timmy and Kestrel but Doc said to give them menus too. This surprised other diners seated near by for of course they were looking and listening to learn what they could about this unusual group.

While Doc and his group ate their delicious dinner they carried on a lively conversation about the ship, its diverse entertainment, the number of people it took to maintain the ship, its length and many other features they were curious about. Dodo was very excited because he had been allowed in the engine room and was eager to tell Doc all he had learned. Dodo had been given this privilege because the Doc was an old friend of the Captain. They all listened to Dodo and questioned him when he talked about fuel per nautical mile and those things only Dodo or Doc understood. Suzy and Kestrel had a hard time to suppress laughter when they saw the astonished faces on the Toobig listeners. Suzy was sure they would ask Doc something about what they heard and sure enough they did. Doc simply had not been going to spoil the evening by telling the four to talk like little children so he had an answer ready. Several Toobigs hurried to leave the dining room before Doc's group so they could stop at Doc's table and say hello and just seem to be polite but not nosy, which of course they were.

The Toobigs all spoke in about the same manner. After saying good evening it went something like, my what a wonderful family you have and we couldn't help over hearing how much knowledge they have, they appear so gifted, where do you live and where do they go to school.

Doc ended all questions and remarks saying, "I believe in starting teaching at a very young age, thank you and good evening."

Finally they were left alone. Doc then took them to the theater to see a Disney movie.

It had been a wonderful day and they were all ready to go to bed. When they reached the cabin Timmy put on his pajamas and started to go out on the balcony when Doc said he thought it was rather late. Timmy decided he should tell Doc and Dodo about Aquila visiting the ship in Seattle and saying he was going to follow and be ready to help. Timmy wanted to go out to see if maybe he would visit again. Doc wasn't very surprised and told him to go ahead and in the morning he should also tell Suzy and Kestrel. Timmy stepped out and found Aquila perched on the railing. They were both happy to be together and Timmy told Aquila all they had done and also about the Orca whales he had wished he could visit. Aquila assured him he had seen the whales and if he saw them again he would inform them of Timmy's wish. Who knew but what some day they could help the Kin, he thought. He assured Timmy he would always be near and then flew back to the coast to find a nice perch in a tall evergreen where he would spend the night.

The next morning at breakfast Timmy said, "Suzy Q, I have something to tell you and Kestrel."

Suzy groaned and replied, "Timmy you have been doing so good why did you forget?"

For a minute Timmy couldn't figure out what he forgot until he thought of what he had just said.

Timmy slapped his forehead and rolled his eyes in his typical I'm sorry mode and then said, "A thousand apologies for the Q."

Suzy and Kestrel laughed at his antics and then Timmy told them about Aquila. They were very happy to hear this, for there were lots of ways Aquila could help when they went ashore.

The Kin were all on the balcony eagerly watching as the ship made its way to dock at the port of Juneau Alaska. They looked forward to seeing Juneau as it was the capital of Alaska, but more than that was the thought of finding a clue to Timmy's missing parents.

The day in the town was spent roaming the streets and sight seeing and all the time they were listening to the natives gossiping, hoping to hear an odd remark or comment that may be a clue. As evening approached they wearily walked back to the ship. When they reached their cabin they all seemed to have the same feeling about this not being where Timmy's parents, the Dubars, had left the ship. At dinner they talked about how they were expecting a big city and it was rather disappointing to find this little town the capital of Alaska. Suzy said she thought a state capital should be large and impressive, to which all agreed.

The ship left port on schedule and the next stop was Skagway. The Kin travelers sat on the balcony until it was quite late. They all secretly seemed to feel this was their last night on board even though Doc had booked passage to Anchorage. Timmy was telling his friends what he had heard about the small town of Hanes located close to Skagway. He had learned that just out of town, at the Chilkot Bald Eagle Preserve, existed the worlds' largest concentration of bald eagles. He said he had heard that groves of cottonwood trees, along the Chilkot river, were loaded with eagles and the river was full of salmon. Timmy ended his bit of information with these words,

"Boy, wouldn't Aquila like that, he would have lots of friends and could catch a meal of salmon whenever he wanted it."

Aquila perched near, but unseen in the shadows, heard Timmy and was happy to know he was thinking of him. Aquila hoped he had time to visit this place.

Morning arrived sunny and warm and shortly after breakfast Doc and the four Kin left the ship as soon as it docked in Skagway. They roamed up and down and at noon went into a small café on Main Street. They had ordered lunch, it had been served and they were quietly eating when the two men in the next booth started talking so loud they were easily heard.

The first man to speak was quite old and very scruffy looking. He had uncombed hair and a scraggly beard. He was dressed in jeans and a red plaid shirt. "Well, well, here comes old man Nugget with his donkey. I haven't seen him in town for several months. Wonder what he's in town for?"

His companion, a skinny young man in a red flannel shirt and bib overalls, answered, "He probably ran out of coffee, flour or salt for that's about all he buys."

Scruffy laughed and said, "Or baking powder. Jake, the guy at the waterfront grocery where Nugget shops, says that all he talks about is his great baking powder biscuit cook, as if he had a cook."

Skinny replied, "Well you know that sure is strange, and of course we know he is odd, but he often talks about his cook being so short that he had to make a special stand so she could reach everything. He really has got an imagination, and he'd have to, to name a donkey a blame fool name like "Iggy Wando".

When the words Iggy Wando were said, Doc and the four tiny people were stunned. They believed that no one outside their village could know those words except the Dubars. They all looked out the window to see what the old man looked like and where he was going. They finally reacted and rose as one. They had to talk to this man, but Doc said they should give him a minute to question the men in the next booth. They sat back down and Doc stepped to the next booth, introduced himself and asked if they knew the old man who had just walked by.

Scruffy, while scratching his beard, answered, "Not really, mostly gossip. You probably could get your best information from Jake at his store. Nugget usually spends the night in town and sleeps in Jakes' storeroom"

Skinny then told him how to get to Jake's store. Doc thanked them and seeing they looked curious he said he would like to take a picture of the old man and his mule as a memento of his Alaska trip. Scruffy advised him to stay away from the old man as he was touchy and accused everyone of spying on him. Doc thanked them for the advice and then they all left the café.

Timmy was so excited he wanted to chase the old man down at once but Doc said he thought the best idea was that he take the four of them back to the ship and then he would ask his friend the

Captain for advise and go to the store later. Though Timmy was reluctant they did as Doc wished.

Doc took his crew to their cabin and then rushed to see the Captain. It was decided Doc and the Captain would go to the store at dusk, for that was when most people were home eating dinner, and they hoped there would be no customers in the store. Doc went back to his cabin and explained this and suggested they order food and eat on the balcony.

They had their dinner and it was time for Doc to leave. It seemed to those waiting he was gone for hours, but it was only a little more than one. When he returned he told them he had talked to Jake and what he had learned. No one knew the old man's real name, but they called him Nugget because when he came to town he had a gold nugget he wore on a watch chain and always had gold dust to pay for his purchases. The natives suspected he panned for gold in streams near old mines to get enough to live on for he never had very much with him. He was very suspicious and accused people of following him and spying to get his gold. Jake believed he lived somewhere over White's Pass, maybe in The Yukon, Canadian Territory near Lake Dezadeash. Nobody really knew but people had seen him and his mule in that area as they traveled Highway Two. He also came from that direction when he visited town. Jake said he never talked much but did ramble on some times about his little cook and helper. He figured because Nugget lived alone for months at a time he probably had imaginary companions like children sometimes did. Jake said Nugget would stay a day or two sleeping in his storage shed. Jake then asked why Doc was asking about Nugget. Doc told Suzy and the others he hated to lie but he knew finding the Dubars was more important and it wasn't a lie that would hurt anyone so he told Jake he had seen the man and he looked like an old prospector and he thought he may have some interesting stories to tell. Jake said that he didn't think Nugget would talk to anyone, but if Doc came back alone the next day he would introduce him as a friend. He went on to say the Captain better not come a long as Nugget didn't like anyone that wore a fancy uniform. Police were all right Nugget claimed but not fancy uniforms, then Jake shook his head and said he just couldn't figure out Nugget.

When Doc finished talking, everyone was excited for they were sure Nugget's cook and helper were Timmy's parents. They didn't want to think of going to bed but Doc said they should all get a good nights sleep as the ship was leaving the next afternoon and they had to decide if they were going to go on or stay here. He said if they stayed here they would have to pack up lots of their clothes, leave them with the Captain and probably just take very sturdy clothes and shoes. This all would have to be decided by lunchtime. They said they would go to bed and hope to sleep. Timmy asked if he could sleep on the balcony, this perhaps being their last night on the ship. He was given permission and though every one was nervous over what would happen the next day, they finally were all asleep.

The next morning as Doc prepared to go to the store, Timmy asked to go along. He said he wouldn't say a word and just pretend to be Doc's little boy. Doc could tell it meant a lot to Timmy, to see this man who may know of his parents, so he agreed to take him along. During the night he had decided this is where they would leave the ship so he asked Suzy, Kestrel and Dodo if they would sort every ones clothes. He told them to put the formal clothes, sandals and unnecessary items in one large suitcase to be left with the Captain. Kestrel, being the adult and with more knowledge of living under all kinds of conditions, was left in charge.

Doc and Timmy left the ship and started for the store. It was a beautiful day with the sun sparkling on the waves, the sea gulls calling and Doc was sure he saw Aquila in the distance, but Timmy, who usually noticed and enjoyed all things seemed unaware of everything, even missing Aquila flying overhead.

When the two arrived at the store, Nugget was just coming out of the storeroom. To Timmy the man looked enormous, though he was really only about six feet tall. He had let his dark hair and beard grow very bushy and this added to his huge and scary appearance. Doc said hello to Jake and Jake called to Nugget to come meet Doc Raldo. As he approached, Timmy hid behind Doc.

Nugget strolled over and said "Howdy" and shook Doc's hand.

Doc replied, "Hello, I hear you live out in the country somewhere. I was wondering if you could tell us what Alaska is like in the wilderness?"

Nugget looked at Doc to see if he was serious or just another nosey outsider. He decided he liked Doc's looks so he started talking, "Well, its pretty hard to say, it can be very dangerous what with the snow in winter and the bears always near the rivers grabbing salmon when ones fishing." He was about to continue when he saw a tiny child peering out from behind Doc.

"Who is he?" Nugget asked.

Doc, bending down and putting his arm around the boy, replied "This is my little son Timmy."

Nugget mumbled, "Don't think so," and walked away and out the door.

Doc started to follow but Jake said, "Better not."

Doc and Jake couldn't figure what had happened but Jake thought it must be about Timmy and figured Nugget probably didn't like children, as he recalled in the years he'd known Nugget he had never seen him glance at a child even if they were running around him in the store. One thing he did know he told Doc and that was he could be sure Nugget wouldn't speak to him again after leaving like that. Hearing Jakes last comments Doc and Timmy started back to the ship.

CHAPTER TWENTY-TWO

When Nugget left the store he didn't go far, as he wanted to see where Doc and the boy went. He was so disappointed, for he had liked the looks of Doc and he had liked few men in his life. Doc had lied to him. He knew that was not Doc's boy. He knew because he looked just like the man and woman he had locked in his cabin in the woods. He would have to follow them! They must know something he thought or they wouldn't be spying on him. He followed them staying at a distance, so they wouldn't see him. He saw them board the ship and he sat down behind some boxes. He wasn't sure what to do next, but decided to watch them until the ship left port. He wanted to be sure they sailed for Anchorage. He sat on the dock for over an hour until he saw the ship's crew preparing for the ship's sailing. He figured he was safe and was about to leave when he couldn't believe his eyes. Doc, the tiny boy and three children were walking down the gangplank carrying suitcases! Now knowing they were staying in Skagway he knew he must follow them to see where they were going. He knew he must find a way to grab Timmy. Again he trailed along behind them as they made their way toward the only nice hotel in town. He saw them check in and knew they would be staying at least one night. Now he had some time to work on a plan. He went back to the store.

Jake asked him, "Been out for a walk?"

Nugget answered, "Yep and the town is as dull as ever. Guess I'll do my shopping and get old Iggy Wando packed up, then I'll go have a steak dinner at Mom's Café and head for home."

"What, not staying another night?" asked Jake.

"Maybe," said Nugget. "Do you mind leaving the room in back unlocked in case I do? I'll pay."

"Don't worry about paying, I'll leave it open. Now what are you needing to buy?"

Nugget made his purchases, packed them tightly in a large canvas bag and took them with him as he went to feed his donkey. He kept his donkey, which he had purchased years ago from an old prospector, in a lean to shed on the edge of town, which was rented to him for a small fee. Nugget gave the donkey some water and grain. He left his purchases in the shed, locked the door and went back to town to have his favorite meal he always ate when coming to town. When he had finished eating it was getting dark so he decided he could probably go near the hotel, where Doc was staying, without being seen. He cautiously sneaked around the building until he found a spot near the front door that was well out of sight, due to some kind of large evergreen. Nugget sat down to wait. He did not know just what he was waiting for but he wanted to learn, if he could, what Doc was doing.

Doc and the Kin were now settled in three rooms. Doc had a room to himself and the other four had come to his room for a meeting. Everyone had suggestions about what to do but the only one they agreed on was that they should go to bed early, get a good rest, get up early in the morning and pack things for leaving at any time. The meeting ended and they went out to dinner.

Nugget saw them go and he stayed where he was. His only hope was to catch Timmy alone.

Nugget heard the five coming back to the hotel for they were talking and laughing quite loudly. They went in but still Nugget sat hidden and waited. As he sat waiting he tried to think through all that had occurred since he had crashed his plane in the Alaskan wilderness. About ten years ago he had made a terrible mistake, agreeing to fly for some smugglers. His plane had developed engine trouble and he had crashed with a full load of contraband. He had not been injured but the plane was a wreck and nothing could be salvaged. Fearing his bosses would blame him and want to get even for their lost goods, he fled into the nearby mountains. As the years passed he slowly became afraid of every stranger. During one monthly trip to Skagway he went to pick up his donkey in the lean-to only to find the little couple huddled in the far corner. Immediately he was sure they were sent to find him. He wouldn't listen when they had begged him to let them go, telling him they were from the states. He grabbed them and threw them in his big gunnysack and tied them to the saddle of his donkey. He had been keeping them prisoners in his log house in the mountains ever since.

Now he wondered if he could have been wrong, for these people with the small boy were from the states. He also wondered if maybe they were just searching for the little couple. Maybe he had talked too much around town about his cook and that's what led them to him. And maybe no one else was looking for him. There were so many "maybes" his head began to hurt and he thought the only way to find all the answers was to kidnap the tiny boy and worry about what to do after that. For if he had been wrong he was really in trouble. Of course he didn't know the small folks were kin and not known about by the Americans. If he had he wouldn't have worried as he was doing, for his fear was that if they were from the lower forty-eight states he would be hunted for kidnapping.

Doc saw Suzy and Kestrel safely to their room for the night then he stopped at Dodo and Timmy's room to say goodnight before going to his room.

Dodo hurriedly prepared for bed and told Timmy he should do the same. Timmy sat on the edge of his bed talking about Aquila and wondering if he knew where they were and saying he should go out and check if he could see him. Dodo told him to shush and go to sleep but Timmy kept on chattering until Dodo didn't answer anymore. Timmy asked him a question and when there was no response he knew Dodo was asleep. Timmy wanted so much to see Aquila he decided to slip outside and look around. He thought, just five minutes, no one will know. He soon learned he had made a bad decision.

Timmy quietly slipped out of the room, and down the hall to the front door, then outside where he stepped into the shadow of an evergreen tree.

As Nugget sat reminiscing, he heard a slight noise and there was the boy he wanted, just three feet from him. He took his jacket he'd been using to lean his head on, and as Timmy turned, thinking to see Aquila, Nugget dropped the jacket over Timmy and picked him up. Poor Timmy, between the surprise and the smothering jacket he couldn't make a sound or move.

Nugget was up and running, back behind the hotel and through an alley before Timmy could try to make an effort of any kind. He soon knew it was no use to struggle. The man was too strong. He knew it was Nugget even though he hadn't been able to see him. It was hard for him to breathe with his head all wrapped tight and he wondered how long the man would keep running. Finally he stopped and as he set Timmy down he told him not to make a sound or some one would get hurt. He took the jacket off and when he did he immediately put tape across Timmy's mouth. Timmy looked up and saw it was indeed Nugget and he didn't feel the least afraid. Nugget rapidly loaded the donkey with his supplies. He tied everything on so there was a place on top where he could set Timmy. He covered Timmy with a blanket, all but his face, and also tied him on. Nugget then took the donkey's bridal and started walking.

The only words Nugget spoke were, "Lets go home Iggy Wando," which made the donkey twitch his ears and give a soft bray.

Nugget and the donkey walked at a swift pace even though by now they were traveling by moonlight. Timmy tried to stay awake as they traveled on and on hoping he could later recognize the path. He soon knew he couldn't see well enough to learn anything and he fell asleep. He awoke when the donkey stopped walking. Looking about he saw it would soon be daylight. They were at the mouth of a cave and he guessed they were about to make camp.

Nugget lifted Timmy down and then took the tape off his mouth. He told Timmy to take the blanket and go sit in the cave. He did as he was told and Nugget led the donkey in the cave and took the pack off his back. He took some rolls and cheese from a sack, handed some to Timmy and took some for himself.

He gave Timmy some water and then told him he should rest. He took a blanket for himself and lay down across the mouth of the cave to sleep. Because the entrance to the cave was narrow, neither Timmy nor the donkey could get out of the cave without waking Nugget.

CHAPTER TWENTY-THREE

Doc Raldo rose at dawn and after dressing he knocked to see if Suzy and Kestrel were awake. He found them all ready to go so they all went to the boys' room.

Dodo had just finished dressing in a hurry. He was so upset when he answered Doc's knock he could hardly talk but he did manage to say, "Timmy is gone!"

Doc, Suzy and Kestrel shoved into the room saying, how, when, where. Dodo told them about Timmy talking on and on about Aquila the night before and how he finally fell asleep while Timmy was still talking. Dodo figured Timmy must have gone out to see if Aquila was near and been kidnapped, perhaps by Nugget.

Doc wanted to know why he thought Timmy had been gone all night. Dodo told them to look at Timmy's bed to see if it had been slept in. It was still just the way it had been made. Doc had to agree about that but said they should check around first because maybe he had been locked out. Dodo said his door had not been locked when he opened it for Doc. Now they all rather agreed with Dodo so Doc said they should go have breakfast and then go to Jake's store to learn if Nugget was still here.

Jake was just opening his store when they arrived and was surprised to see Doc with three young people. He wondered where the tiny boy was that had been with Doc yesterday. Doc said he was there to see Nugget so Jake went to get him. When he came back he told Doc that Nugget had left and it looked like he had gone the evening before. Doc thanked him and they started to leave before Jake would question what he wanted. Jake sensed there was something wrong that they wanted to keep quiet and he was a pushover when children were involved.

Jake called to Doc, "Wait a minute."

Doc turned and said, "I'm really in a hurry."

Jake hesitated, then said, "Since the ship is gone and you're still here I think perhaps you have troubles. I don't want to know what they are but I think being a stranger here you may need help. I don't want those youngsters with you hurt. I know a little old man, named Joe, who has been here for years and I know some of those he has helped. He never tells of his help to others, but those helped tell the stories. You can tell him anything, and he won't repeat it. I know because he helped me when I first arrived here as a scared young kid. Please talk to him before you do anything else. Go for a walk on the beach, I'll see that he finds you."

Jake's remarks so surprised Doc he barely thought to mumble a thank you as he left the store. Doc and the three walked a block before talking it over and deciding to go down to the beach. They walked away from the town. After going quite a distance they sat down on a log to talk.

They discussed what Jake had said and that if the man was small, maybe he was Kin. This so excited Suzy and Dodo that no one noticed the man approaching until he spoke.

He said in a soft voice, "I'm Joe. Jake sent me. If you're wondering did I hear your remarks, yes I did, but what I hear or learn I never repeat. No, I'm not Kin nor do I know what Kin is, but I'm aware of unseen helping hands. I was helped so that is why I help. Do you wish to tell me why Jake thought you needed me?"

The group looked up in surprise and saw before them a smallish person, about five feet tall. He was dressed all in buckskins with moccasins on his small feet. He had snow-white hair, a wrinkled face that was a map of kindness. His eyes twinkled as he smiled at all of them.

Doc hesitated a minute, and when the others nodded yes to Joe's question, he told him they had to find Nugget for they were sure he had kidnapped their little friend Timmy. They asked if he knew where Nugget lived and how to get there. Joe did not ask any questions or why they suspected kidnapping. He said he thought he knew about where Nugget lived. It was somewhere just over White Pass near the large Lake Dezadeash. When they heard this information they were ready to leave.

Joe stopped them when he said, "Not so fast, what are your plans?"

Suzy spoke, before her Dad could answer. "No plans now, we'll just get on the bus that goes to White Pass and get off at the pass. We will make our plans on the bus."

Doc said, "Suzy you should stop and think, we can't just rush off, we have to act more responsibly. No thinking is what may have got Timmy in trouble."

Joe agreed with Doc and then asked if he should say how he thought they should proceed.

They all said, "Please do."

He said there was no big hurry as Nugget would take two or three days to walk to the summit, which was a little over three thousand feet and the way was hard to climb. That would give them time to plan. He thought if Doc had the money he should ask Jake to find him an old car to rent, or buy, and preferably a jeep, or a truck. With a jeep he could get off the highway if he wanted to and drive on one of several trails toward the lake. This way he could hide the car by covering with brush and it was quite likely no one would touch it. He would then have a way back. Next he should pack only two sets of clothing for each, one set in waterproof plastic bags so they would always have something dry to wear. It would be good for each to have a backpack with rations, matches and water bottles. They should wear warm jackets, gloves and rain gear. They should leave in about three days and he would go along if they wished and help them hunt for Nugget's home.

After Joe was finished with all his instructions they were all so glad Jake had sent him. Doc was sure they would now have a chance to find Timmy. They thanked Joe and told him he must go along for they now knew how much they needed his knowledge. He looked pleased and then told them to do their best at getting ready and he would meet them at Jakes' in three days.

Doc didn't worry about rain gear or backpacks for he had bought school backpacks and child's rain gear for Dodo and Suzy in Seattle, when he had planned for the possibility of leaving the ship. Knowing Timmy, he hadn't bothered about gear for him. He had worried about Kestrel though for as tiny as she was, she insisted on an adult status. He had confided in granny Dubar and she had made a miniature green rain cape and a tiny backpack. Doc had found tiny boots and mittens in a child's shop in Seattle.

The next two days were busy for all and Suzy and Kestrel spoke often of Aquila, wondering where he was. It was just daylight on the third morning, after Timmy's disappearance when Suzy awoke and opened the curtains to look out. The first thing she saw was Aquila perched on the roof of the next building. She looked out and seeing no one around she opened her window and Aquila flew to her. Aquila seemed very agitated and Suzy was so shaken she forgot all Timmy had been teaching her ever since her encounter with the deer. She knew learning what Aquila knew, now depended solely on her, and she just couldn't think clearly. Kestrel had awakened and guessed what Suzy was going through. She jumped out of bed went over to Suzy and whispered "Igy wando iffel giffle." It was the help Suzy needed. She had a natural ability to communicate with animals but Timmy had shown her how, by nods sounds and gestures to make known questions, and further her ability. Suzy was now ready to hear from Aquila. He was very distraught for he had lost Timmy. He had seen Nugget grab Timmy from the front of the hotel and he had followed them ever since, but this morning they were just gone. They had entered a mineshaft, he thought for the night, but he never saw them leave. This was near the top of the mountain. Suzy then communicated to Aquila that they were quite sure they knew where Nugget was going and they were about to follow him in a car, so Aquila should follow the car. They would again share what they knew the first night they left the highway. Aquila then flew off before people started getting up.

Doc's party collected their luggage and loaded the jeep that Doc had bought. After breakfast they went to Jake's. Joe was waiting there with extra gear and after all was packed they drove off heading for White Pass.

As they traveled up Highway Two they wondered about all the Klondike gold seekers who had climbed this way on the old Chilkoot trail. Dodo had read the history of this trail. He said these seekers were called "Cheechakos", meaning tenderfeet, and in 1898 the Royal Northwest Mounted Police had decreed each man must bring to the Klondike a years supply of goods. Joe added the information that this was about two thousand pounds per man and they had to make many trips up and back as they had to carry it all on their backs and could only take about two hundred pounds each trip.

Everyone really enjoyed Dodo's history lesson and with added information from Joe they marveled at how men could have made the steep climb. Talking about the gold rush and the early days of Skagway made the trip up to the Yukon go faster and kept the group from worrying about Timmy.

CHAPTER TWENTY-FOUR

Timmy would have been enjoying this journey if he hadn't known he was causing Doc and his friends to worry. The area wasn't much different from where he lived and often he would see a bear or a deer. There did seem to be more wild creatures here than in the Olympic Mountains and he thought he glimpsed a moose and a big horn sheep. He wished he had a chance to converse with them. After the first night and part of the next day they traveled only during the day. He thought it was because Nugget was no longer afraid of being followed. Timmy saw an eagle circling overhead at different times during the first two days. He knew it was Aquila because they had agreed on a certain flight action as a signal. It was now the third day, almost noon, and Timmy had not seen Aquila and this worried him. He hoped it only meant he had flown back to alert Doc and his friends and he had not lost sight of them.

Nugget had stopped the past night at another cave and there they had their meal and spent the night. The next morning, rather then leave the cave, he had led them farther into it. He used a flashlight inside the shaft and after a half hour they came out of the cave lower down on the mountainside where the cave opening was hidden by a big bush. They traveled all day and stopped at dusk in a dense stand of trees near a stream. Timmy was now upset because he was sure Aquila had lost sight of them due to the trip through the caves. Nugget no longer tied Timmy though he watched him closely. He couldn't know that Timmy would not try to escape, because he was sure he would see his Mom and Dad at the end of the journey.

Timmy strolled over to the little donkey and started petting him. He heard a whisper.

"Don't look so sad, it will be fine, he will never hurt you."

Timmy couldn't believe he had heard right. He looked all about then back at the donkey and he knew this was his new friend. He put his arms around the neck of his new friend and softly said, "Iggy Wando."

The next morning Nugget got them started early and he walked faster than usual. He only took a few minutes for lunch and hurried on. Late in the day he went through thick brush and under low branches and as he continued this, Timmy, wise in the ways of his people, knew that Nugget was hiding his trail.

Just before dark they entered a small open place in the thick forest and before them, Timmy saw a small log house. The thought of his parents being in this house made him start to shake. Nugget noticed this but thought the boy was just cold. He wrapped him in a blanket and carried him to the house. He unlocked the door and set him inside. Timmy had been preparing himself to show no surprise, in front of Nugget, no matter who or what he saw.

It was quite dark in the cabin with the only light from an oil lamp. Timmy couldn't see very well.

Nugget spoke, "Get us some food, we are cold and hungry."

At his words, Tish and Bern Dubar jumped up from a low bench that was in the shadows.

Nugget removed the blanket that was engulfing Timmy and the Dubars upon seeing Timmy, were too stunned to move.

Nugget laughed at this and said, "Yep, I found another one. I knew cause he looked just like you two. Now you'll have help. Well, get busy."

Tish and Bern went to get food. They whispered to each other about the stranger but they were sure it was their Timmy, come to find them.

Timmy did his best to hide his feelings for after one glance he knew it was his parents and he thought they had recognized him. He thought for now it was best to act like they were strangers.

Tish hurried and made biscuits and when they were ready she and Bern served them with bowls of stew which had been cooking all day. The heat from the little cook stove made the cabin warm and cozy. Though it was now July it was very cool here at night. While they ate no one spoke and Timmy looked about the cabin. It was one big room and he could see into two others where the doors were ajar. What little he could see, from where he sat, one looked like a bathroom. This didn't surprise him for he knew how the Kin had used water, piped from springs, in their village. His big question was why hadn't his parents left. He knew his Dad could talk with animals so they needn't be afraid in the forest. He kept looking about and finally, though the light was dim, he saw the metal bars on the windows. Now he saw the place was like a jail. With big log walls, floors and outside door and that door locked and barred it would be impossible to leave.

Nugget had taken care of the donkey and brought the pack from his back into the cabin while dinner was being made, locking the door every time he stepped out. He now opened the pack, put the groceries away, and the last two items he put on the table in front of Tish.

"For you," Nugget said.

He abruptly said, "Good night" and went in the other room and closed the door and they heard the lock click.

Timmy started to speak but Tish put her fingers to her lips meaning silence. They sat this way until after all was quiet in Nugget's room and they could hear the faint sound of snoring.

The Dubars now spoke at the same time, saying "Timmy?"

Timmy could only answer with the words, "Iggy wondo iffel giffel."

They jumped off their chairs and the next several minutes were spent hugging, kissing and crying.

It took quite some time for them to calm down. At last they were ready to talk and Timmy was asked to tell his story first. It took hours but he told them everything that had happened from the time they were separated until that very minute. He didn't forget to tell that Granny Dubar and all at the village were well. Bern was glad to hear Aquila was near for he bet now the eagle would find them.

Timmy now wanted to hear his parents' story, but they could tell he was really tired from the trip and the excitement of their reunion so they told him it wasn't much of a story. They said Nugget had found them, hiding in a shack in Skagway, after they had managed to get off the ship. He had brought them here, locked them in and they had been here all these years. Details they said they could tell anytime. Timmy was sure he knew where the shack was.

The Dubars had a small bed in a corner of the big room and they put a warm quilt on the floor for Timmy to lay on and several blankets for cover. They showed Timmy the bath and were about to go to bed when Timmy remembered the two packages Nugget gave his mother and he asked her what they could be. She then opened them. There was candy in one and green wool cloth in the other. This surprised Timmy and she told him Nugget had always brought them candy and he had kept her supplied with green material ever since he had found them when they had been wearing their green Hidey Clothes. Tish put the items away and three happy people went to bed.

CHAPTER TWENTY-FIVE

Doc and his party reached the summit of White Pass and soon he or Joe must decide which side trails towards Lake Dezadeash, they should try. They were not in Alaska anymore but in Canada's Yukon Territory. Joe said it didn't matter as people up here went back and forth between the two countries all the time. He had been here once and to the lake and he suggested they watch for a sign reading Lake Dezadeash. He said it had been put up by summer hikers and pointed in the general direction. This seemed as good an idea as any so when the sign appeared Doc turned the Jeep off the highway and on to the rutted trail. Doc was surprised how far he could drive before he ran out of trail and came to a dead end of thick woods. It was getting late in the day so Joe said they should camp for the night and rest.

Aquila had faithfully followed all day, and looked over the landscape but hadn't seen anything unusual. He perched near camp to make Suzy aware of his presence then flew off.

The next morning, breakfast over, Doc and Joe moved the Jeep away from trails end. They found an opening between two trees that was just barely wide enough to go between. Beyond them a few yards, were big bushes to hide the Jeep behind. They took those supplies Joe insisted they needed and put them in their backpacks. They were now ready to leave. Joe kept hesitating, to Doc's dismay.

Doc finally asked, "Joe is there a problem?"

"I'm worried about Kestrel," he said. "It is going to be hard walking and I think Dodo and Suzy will be alright but Kestrel will have trouble keeping up. Now I know she is older than she looks but this trek will be hard."

Kestrel was not surprised at his comments, as she knew he had no idea of their life in the forest and what they could do with the help of different creatures. Wanting to keep Joe from being upset she had an idea.

Kestrel spoke to Joe, "I will stay behind and camp in the jeep."

Now Dodo and Suzy were upset and told Joe and Doc no way would they accept that. Kestrel was going along and as there was no big hurry they would take their time and help Kestrel if she needed help, which they doubted.

Doc agreed fully. No way would he leave Suzy's aunt behind.

Joe accepted the decision and so they started.

Joe took out his compass and led off due west. He found a narrow trail and it was fairly easy walking all morning. They stopped by a small stream for lunch and rested a half hour. As they left the stream they had rough walking until they found another trail. Joe told them the trails were usually made by animals going to a stream to drink. Joe could not know that the Kin already knew this.

As dark approached they looked for a place to camp and soon found a spot they liked. They set up camp and when they sat down to eat, Joe was surprised that Kestrel seemed the one least tired.

They traveled on for five days. Each day was about the same. The fifth day they came to the shores of Lake Dezadeash.

The weather had been nice all the past day, but just as they reached the lake it began to rain. They all ran under a large evergreen tree, the only place to stay fairly dry. Up until now they had been in good spirits, but after traveling miles they had reached the lake and no sign of a human. The pouring rain didn't help and the five just sat under the tree feeling downcast. The Kin took blankets from their packs and curled up for a nap. Soon Doc and Joe did the same.

They woke in late afternoon and much to their delight the sun was shining. The nap and sun made them feel better and they fixed a camp site on the lake shore and started a fire. Joe threw a fish line in the lake and caught a large salmon. Joe cooked the fish on a spit and they all said it was the best they ever ate. They didn't forget Aquila and put some food on a log near where he was perched.

Suzy and Kestrel decided to walk a ways on the beach. They were busy talking and hadn't noticed the big black bear coming towards them. Joe had looked their way and seeing they were unaware he yelled loudly, grabbed the spit for a weapon and was ready to run to them, but Dodo grabbed him and pushed him down. Joe was furious.

He yelled, "What's the matter with you?"

Dodo replied, "Just be quiet and watch."

Doc was near and he too was quiet and watching.

Suzy and Kestrel had heard the yell and they looked around.

Kestrel whispered, "Remember our Timmy, you can do it."

Suzy knew she meant, talk to the bear. Kestrel stopped and Suzy kept walking until the bear was about four feet away. She stopped and so did the bear. She greeted the bear and said she was here looking for a Kin. She was overjoyed when he answered for she wasn't yet sure of her abilities with any creature but Aquila. After a few minutes of talk they nodded to each other and the bear turned and ambled into the water to try to catch a salmon.

Suzy and Kestrel hurried back to camp so Suzy could tell what she had learned.

Suzy said she was told humans had never been seen this far west except in boats on the lake. She was advised the party should walk back east, along the lake shore, for about one day. A huge human had been seen about that distance away, fishing on the edge of a lake. He came often and after fishing he would disappear into the forest.

This knowledge caused the group to again feel good and raise their hopes of success for finding Timmy. No one questioned Suzy's encounter with the bear and Doc was bursting with pride. His daughter had done so well since living with the Kin. She had learned so much and had been fearless in her approach to the bear, though Doc had been aware of her doubt in her ability. The night before she had told her Dad how she felt about what she may be required to do now that Timmy was gone. He had done his best to assure her she would do fine and now she had.

Joe was mystified. Not being Kin he had trouble with what he had seen and heard. He remembered bits of strange tales that native Alaskans had told him and now he believed all he had heard. What he had just seen and heard was similar to the tales, so he had to believe.

Morning arrived and after packing, the party started back along the lake. They walked all day and towards the end of the day they came to a place where it looked like some one may have camped. They stopped and made camp. After eating Suzy walked over to a log near the water. Aquila perched on the log and they talked. Aquila flew away and Suzy heard a voice asking "Are you Kin?' Suzy quickly looked around trying to see who could be speaking.

Again someone spoke, "I won't show myself until you answer. I saw you speak with the eagle and only Kin do that, so are you kin?"

"Yes, yes," said Suzy, "We're from the lower forty-eight states. Please we do need help."

Suzy looked toward the nearest hiding place, a thick bush, and saw two Kin appear. They were both dressed in the traditional green hidey clothes and looked much like Kestrel in height and age.

The oldest looking one spoke, "I am called Suma and this is Kale. Why aren't you dressed in hidey clothes?"

Suzy answered, "I am Suzy and if you will go with me and meet my companions we will answer all your questions."

"But two in your group look like Toobigs, first you must tell us of them," said Suma.

"Don't worry," said Suzy, "one is my father and one is a helper who would never betray us."

Suma and Kale whispered to each other and decided it was safe.

Kale spoke this time, "We'll go to meet your party."

Dodo, Kestrel and Doc were sitting by the fire and Joe was resting near by. They had been busy talking so they hadn't paid attention to Suzy after they looked for her and saw her sitting on the log with Aquila. As she stepped up to the fire and asked them to make room, they were amazed to see the two green clad Kin. They all simply stared until Suzy spoke and introduced them. Doc jumped up and found a small log for them to sit on and Kestrel offered to make tea or get them some water. They both thanked Doc and Kestrel and sat down.

Suzy said she would now keep her promise and answer all their questions. They wanted to know why they were here, where they were from, and why didn't they wear their green hidey suits so they could be recognized by other Kin. Trying to keep the story fairly short Doc told them about Timmy, the hunt for his parents and that having to travel with Toobigs the Kin must dress like Toobigs children.

Suma and Kale could hardly believe two Kin may have been living in these woods for years and they didn't know about them. They said it was very possible though if they had been kept locked up somewhere. They had seen a Toobig fishing in the lake several times, but they had never followed him. They thought he was like all Toobigs who came to the lake to fish and then went back to their towns.

Suma and Kale said they were really happy to see Kin from so far away and their whole village would want to help.

"Tomorrow you must come to our village and meet all who live there." Suma said. He then continued, "We will plan how to search and between us, your eagle friend, and other forest friends of ours we will soon find them."

Everyone was overjoyed after Suma spoke and they thanked him and Kale over and over. They were told to save some of the thanks until after Timmy and his parents were found. They then said their goodnights and with a last see you in the morning, they disappeared into the forest.

Those around the fire talked awhile about the amazing evening, then soon Doc said it was time for bed.

Suma and Kale were sitting on the small log feeding sticks into the embers of the fire, left from the previous night, when

Dodo awoke. He was the first up as usual and very surprised their new friends had been up first.

Dodo greeted them and went for water from a nearby spring. He put it on to boil. Joe got up next and headed to the lake to catch a fish for breakfast. Doc soon arose and coffee was bubbling away when Kestrel and Suzy came out of their small pup tent. A big smile appeared on Suma and Kale's face as Kestrel came out. Doc and Dodo turned to see what was causing such smiles and they had to smile also. Kestrel was dressed in her hidey clothes. Her hair was hid under her cap and she looked like part of the green bushes. No one knew she had brought her Kin clothes, hidden among her things. Doc was really glad she had for he could see it made an impact on Suma and Kale.

They soon had a nice breakfast of fish and biscuits ready. Amidst much chatter and laughter they then prepared for the trip to the Kin village.

The journey to the village took about three hours. The village was hidden almost in the same manner as the Kin village in the Olympics. A short way after leaving the tunnel like approach, where Doc and Joe had to walk bent over, they came upon a man carving. He had what looked like a finished statue, about three feet high, sitting off to one side of where he was working. Suzy, Kestrel and Dodo all saw it at the same time and at the same time exclaimed, "Who knows."

Doc, Suma and Kale, completely surprised, didn't know what to think or what they meant.

Suzy spoke up, "Sorry, Dad I will explain it to all later, but now it would take too long and we wish to meet everyone here."

The Kin on lookout had seen them coming and had notified the villagers. The elders and most of the rest of those in the village came to meet the newcomers.

Suma and Kale introduced the visitors and suggested that they and the villagers go to the play field to talk of the visitors' problems. The field was named because the meeting hall was too low for the Toobigs. Everyone proceeded to the designated place. When all were seated, an elder Kin rose and welcomed them and the whole village echoed the welcome. Doc thanked them for letting him and Joe enter their village and visit with them. He promised they would never break that trust.

Suma rose next and told them the story Doc had told him and Kale. There was much exclamation over the story and wonderment. The elder Kin who first spoke now spoke again and suggested they all spend the day planning how to coordinate a hunt the next day. He offered the visitors a place to rest and said they would be served a meal whenever they wished to eat.

Kestrel, Suzy and Dodo were taken to a lovely little cottage hidden away under a huge tree with over hanging branches. They were given rooms where they could rest and told they were free to walk about the village anytime they wished. Kestrel and Suzy were enchanted with the small beds and other furnishings. The Kin had used sturdy tree limbs for bed posts and fashioned them in pleasing shapes. There were small carved chairs and a rocker. Pretty pictures were made of colored rocks, ferns and feathers. The curtains were made of woven reeds. Small plants in baskets were set on low stands and Kestrel said it seemed a forest wonderland. They both looked about closely for they were thinking about ways to enhance their own homes when returning to them.

After a short rest they decided to look around the village. Dodo stepped out of the house at the same time so they all walked together. The first thing they all wanted to see was the statue they had called "Who Knows". They were excited about it because all three had the same idea at the same time.

The wood carver was working as they walked over to him. They told their names and he replied saying his was Jeb. He was very curious as they studied his carving for he had heard them say who knows. It was a very interesting carving, about three feet tall. The main figure was a being who could be either male or female. There were wings extending from the beings shoulders and it was carved to look like a flowing robe hung from shoulders to feet. There were three small carvings at the foot of the statue. They were not distinct but as one looked they seemed to resemble a deer, a bear and an eagle. As far as the Olympic Kin were concerned, it was perfect.

They finally turned to Jeb and Kestrel said, "We must tell you about 'Who Knows'."

She then told him of the Toobigs of Mini Creek and that when anything happened they couldn't explain, they would say "Who knows". Usually the unexplainable was some help or joke done by the Kin. The Kin had decided someday they would put a "Who Knows" statue in the park. They never thought they could because they didn't know what it should look like until they had seen his carving. They wondered if maybe he would sell it to them.

Jeb was extremely pleased that they wanted his statue and just as excited as they over what they wanted to do. He insisted he give it to them and wanted to carve a base for it and put the words "Who Knows" on the base. Jeb thought it would be nice if they tell this story to all when they gathered at the evening meal. They talked a while longer and then Jeb told them to continue their walk and he would start on the base.

Kestrel, Suzy and Dodo continued their walk and Dodo examined their water system and anything he deemed mechanical. They were surprised when a youngster was sent to get them for the evening meal as time had passed so quickly.

The evening meal was served out doors and when they finished Jeb stood on a bench and called for attention. When it became quiet he asked Suzy to tell about "Who Knows". Now everyone was interested for several had heard or been told about the first words spoken by the visitors.

Suzy told the story and all present were very intrigued. Many Kin said to give them the statue but make them pay for it by telling some of the things that the Toobigs found unexplainable. The Olympic Kin laughed and agreed. The next two hours were spent with story telling. The stories of helping were met with applause while the Veronica doll story and Halloween story were greeted with much laughter. The supply of stories finally ran out and the gathering then broke up. It was agreed that the next morning the hunt for Nugget's home would begin.

CHAPTER TWENTY-SIX

Early the following morning several of the most able young Kin gathered and divided in to three groups. They said it was not necessary to go back west as they knew that area well. They would go in the other three directions and return in two days or less, depending on their findings. The Kin from the Yukon Territory asked the Kin from the Olympics to stay in the village until they returned. Doc, Joe and Dodo wanted very much to go but they were over-ruled. The reason given was that the others knew this area so well and the forest creatures living there, that they would be able to travel faster through some places. Also, their animal talkers, there being one with each group, would not have to worry about strangers scaring the forest creatures.

Suma said, "Perhaps Suzy could find her eagle friend and have him fly back and forth over the forest to also help. He had told his friends of Aquila and they also thought it wise.

The three groups left and the Olympic group knew the time would pass slowly. They asked what work they could help with. After much discussion Kestrel and Suzy went to work in the garden and Joe offered to go fishing. Doc said he would gather and chop wood and Dodo went to help repair and add more pipeline from the springs.

Everyone worked steadily all day so time passed swiftly. At dinner time most went to the playfield. The Villagers had decided that most of them should eat together while they had visitors and because two of them were Toobigs, the tables were again set up there. Everyone kept looking for the ones out hunting for Nugget's home to return, but none came back that evening.

Suzy and Kestrel had trouble going to sleep. They were talking and worrying about Timmy. Finally they slept and morning arrived too soon for these two sleepy ones.

Each returned to the same work as they had done the day before. When they stopped for lunch the first group of Yukon Kin returned. They had covered all their area, talked to the deer, bear and bluejays but no one had seen a large bearded Toobig. It was quite a let down but they would wait for the others before feeling too disappointed.

In mid afternoon the second group returned with the same report as the first group. Every ones' hope was now centered on the third group headed by Suma and Kale.

Once again it was dinnertime, then it was past dinner and starting to get dark. Everyone was on edge as all groups were to come back the second day. Just as some began to worry that something bad had happened, Suma, Kale and the group walked in. They all looked very tired but everyone was smiling and that they believed must be good news.

Suma didn't keep them in suspense, he shouted, "We found Nuggets home and the Dubars are there!"

There never before had been such a ringing shout of joy in this village. Everyone was laughing and hugging each other.

Suma asked for food and a short period of rest for he and his group before they told of their trip.

Several Kin rushed to bring food while others brought fresh water and helped them take off their backpacks. The group ate and rested and Suma was soon ready to tell about all his group had found out on their trek.

Suma spoke, "When we left the village we all questioned each other about where he would go if he wanted to hide. All of us answered the same, "Night Forest." This is a place none of us had ever been as there is no reason to go there. First I think I should explain to our visitors why our grandfathers named it "Night Forest." When some of our grandfathers were young they wanted to learn about the land around them and in conversing with creatures of the forest they heard of these dark woods. Like all young men they must see for themselves. After a full days hike, they arrived in the woods. They camped outside the forest and entered the woods the following morning. Although the sun was bright, the forest was as dark as evening. The trees were immense and they grew so closely together only a little light filtered down through the branches. It was very hard to move about as the forest floor was covered with huge ferns, skunk cabbage, rotted fallen trees, bushes and vines. The Kin's' size helped them for they could crawl through small tunnels made by the animals. After some time they came to a small opening in the trees where the sun appeared but they continued on into the forest and finally arrived at a larger opening where there was a small brook formed by a spring. Here there were several large boulders and the ground was stony which may have been why there was less vegetation with only a few stunted trees. They spent the night here and the next day slowly made their way back out of the forest. They judged it probably was at least four miles around. They said they never went back as there was nothing there for the Kin in this 'Night Forest,' and that was how it was named.

Suma stopped speaking to take a sip of water and then he continued, "Night Forest was in our search area so we all decided to start there. Our reason was that a Toobig, with the tools and chain saws we have seen them use, could easily cut his way through the dense brush. Then he could easily hide his trail as we do. Back in the forest he could build a log house and no one would know he was there as Toobigs only come into this area for the lake and fishing. We also thought if he should find the open space and spring he would have his biggest necessity, water.

The first day we traveled fast, not even stopping for lunch so by early afternoon we were in the forest and after an hours struggle through underbrush we hit a very small open space. We couldn't believe our luck. We stopped to rest a few minutes and eat. We were wondering if this was the same spot our grandfathers found and then judged it to be, for we were sitting on a flat stone buried deep in the ground and remembered their account of this small open space. We now had to decide which way to go. At first we couldn't make up our minds and then Aquila arrived from above. He lit and, questioned by Kale, said he had been hunting us since we entered the forest. In flying back and forth above the forest he had seen a thin wisp of smoke. He wanted to lead us to it, but knowing we couldn't see him because of the trees, he had a plan. He would fly low and stop often in a tall evergreen and give the normal call of eagles. This call would not be out of place in the forest and we were to try to follow. The calls kept us going the right way and we made pretty good time. When Aquila made his last call he repeated it at once so we took it as a warning. It was good we did for in a few minutes we saw sunlight and there before us was a fair size open place and on one wide side a log house."

Suma again stopped talking as his throat was feeling dry and scratchy. He asked Kale if he would tell the rest.

Kale, only too happy to tell of their triumph, continued, "We backed away into the forest and made plans. We would go in groups of two, one to the front, one to the back and one to the other side. We would look closely at the building to see if we could get in and watch for movement. We would be back at the starting point in fifteen minutes. When we were back together, group one said there was nothing behind the house but the spring and there were iron bars on the one window. Group two found a big boulder at the end of the house near a window also with bars. They climbed the side away from the house stopping below the top. They peeked around the top and saw a small figure in green working at a kitchen sink. It looked like a female and she was standing on something. Suma and I were watching the front of the house when the door opened and a Toobig came out. He immediately locked the door and went to a small shed. He took a pail from the shed, walked behind the house, returned with water and then put it and some dried grass in the shed. We caught a glimpse of an animal in the shed. The Toobig then went back in the house. The Toobig was large and had a grisly beard. After we all reported what we had seen we knew we had found the right man. We didn't know of any more we could do and it was almost dark so we started back the way we came. We hadn't gone far before we knew we must stop for the night for we could no longer see the trail we had marked. In the morning we started for home. We traveled as fast as we could, after the exhausting day before. All we could think of was telling our visitors the good news."

When Kale finished speaking there was total silence for a moment. Then the cheering began and soon Doc raised his hands for silence. He expressed sincere thanks and appreciation to all who had been looking for Nugget.

Suma accepted the thanks, saying it was just Kin duty and Aquila was the true hero. He then said he thought it would be best to meet in the morning and make plans, for tonight it was best to rest and just think about it.

CHAPTER TWENTY-SEVEN

A meeting of Doc's group and several Yukon Kin was held after breakfast. There was much discussion about what to do and a plan was settled on. Only Suma, Kale and Dodo would go to the "Night Forest" for if their plan worked they wouldn't need more Kin. Dodo was to go so Timmy would see someone he knew. Suma was the leader as he made good quick decisions when necessary. Kale was the animal communicator. The plan was to carry enough supplies for a week. If they weren't back by then the Kin would bring more supplies and check on them. In debating what to do it had been remembered that Kin had seen Nugget fishing in Lake Dezadeash and he usually stayed over night. They were going to do nothing when they got to Nugget's house but watch it for a week, if necessary, and hope that sometime he would go fishing. If not they would stay until he did. When the question of opening a locked door came up, Suma remembered seeing Nugget leave the key in the lock when he went to the shed and they had to hope this was his regular habit.

The rest of the morning was spent getting the trio outfitted. It took some time to find a green suit that would fit Dodo, but after much asking about, one was found.

They were ready to leave by noon and their last request for help was to Suzy. They wanted her to ask Aquila to fly over the area they would be in and to tell him, if he was needed, Kale would loudly give an eagles distress call. Feeling they were now well prepared they bid goodbye and left.

This trek was through an unknown area to Dodo so he had many questions and the time passed swiftly. By late afternoon they were at the edge of "Night Forest" so they decided to camp and leave early the next day.

The evening meal was a pleasant time as Dodo told stories of his village and about Doc and how he came to be with them. Suma and Kale told stories of the Yukon and Alaska Kin. In so doing they gave each other ideas for their villages.

Morning arrived sunny and warm. The three packed up and entered the forest. It was too hard to travel and talk going through this area so not much was said until they reached the first open space. Aquila flew over and called to let them know he was near. They rested a while and then continued by following the marked trail they had made. By late afternoon they arrived close enough to Nugget's house that Dodo got a look at it. After a quick look Suma motioned them back in the forest. They looked about until they found a hidden hollow at the base of a huge tree and made a camp for the week. It was near the spring and a pleasant spot, except for the lack of sunlight or moonlight reaching it. They quietly prepared a meal and soon were sound asleep in their bedrolls.

The call of an eagle awoke them at dawn and they realized how very wise Aquila was. He knew what they were going to watch for and had alerted the three knowing that if Nugget left to fish, it would be early. This early morning alert set the course for the following days. The three figured the morning was the most important time to watch closely as it didn't seem likely Nugget would leave late in the day to travel to the lake.

The three Kin took turns watching the house in the mornings but usually, spent the afternoon exploring or playing games they would make up. Sometimes late in the day they would follow the brook until they were out of sight of the house and take a swim. The water was quite cold but the quick dip was both cleansing and fun. Five days went by in this manner. The only activity they saw was when Nugget came out to tend the donkey and chop wood or just gather branches from the wood pile.

The sixth morning Aquila gave three sharp calls. Suma, Kale and Dodo responded with quiet speed. They were dressed and at their lookouts in minutes, for they were sure Aquila must have seen something unusual.

It was just getting daylight when they saw Nugget lead the donkey from the shed. He led him to the door step where he had several bundles. He put these on the donkeys back and tied them down. He unlocked the door to the house, stepped in for a minute, and as he came back out they heard him say he was leaving. He locked the door. He didn't leave the key in the door this time but hung it on a branch in a near by tree. For a moment their hopes were high, but then they saw Nugget add a padlock. Silently they were saying, "Please, please hide this key too." Later when they talked of this incident they believed it had been the power of their combined concentration or Kin magic that caused the next action.

Nugget started to put the key in his pocket, then he paused and after a minute he walked a few feet and placed the key in a small notch on a log of the house wall. He then gathered up the rope, by which he led the donkey, and walked off across the open space.

The three watching were very tense but followed their plan. Suma and Dodo were to wait ten minutes before going to unlock the door. Kale was to follow Nugget for enough distance to discover how he left the forest. They wanted to learn his trail for they thought it must be easier to travel than the way they came.

Dodo knew when the ten minutes were up for Doc had given him a watch before the trip and Doc had given his own to Suma to use. When the ten minutes were up Dodo ran to get the two keys. He then ran to the door and unlocked both locks. Dodo being a Big could reach the lock and the bent metal strap that was used as a doorknob, but the door opened out and it was too big and too heavy for him to open. Suma and Kale, who had just returned from following Nugget, were both too short. The three were wondering what to do next when Dodo saw a round rock near by and suggested they try to roll it close to the door. With much effort they got it near the door and Suma and Kale climbed up on it and tried to help Dodo pull, but they just weren't strong enough. The door opened out instead of in and it was too heavy for them with only that metal strap to hold onto.

Now Dodo was frantic. He put his mouth to the keyhole and yelled, "Timmy, Timmy, its Dodo. Help us. Push on the door! It is unlocked."

The voice did not surprise Timmy at all. He had been expecting it. Now that Nugget had left to go fishing he believed they would come for him. He ran to the door. His parents were in shock, for they hadn't believed a rescue was possible, so it took them a moment to join Timmy. With the added help the door finally opened.

Timmy hugged Dodo and kept saying, "I knew you would find me, I knew you would find me, I just knew it."

Dodo replied, "Hurry we will talk later. We must all leave at once."

CHAPTER TWENTY-EIGHT

Nugget, leading his donkey, headed for the lake to fish. The supplies were running low because he hadn't figured on an extra mouth to feed when he last stocked up. Oh well, he thought he would make an extra trip. Go to Wild Hank's Corner, up north on the highway. He would catch the bus at the trailhead. It would be faster. He thought having Timmy with them was worth the extra trip. He did enjoy the boy's chatter, though he'd never tell him. He stopped to check the ropes around the packs his donkey was carrying when he realized he had left his rod and tackle back at the cabin. Now he'd have to go back for them. He wasn't too upset for when he checked his watch he saw he had only been walking for twenty minutes or so. He led the donkey off the trail and behind some bushes and tied him in a safe place. He would make better time walking back alone.

He spoke softly, "Back soon Iggy Wando."

Going back to his house he walked swiftly. He came around the last curve in the path and saw his door standing open. He saw four figures in green coming out through the door and he let out a loud roar and yelled, "Nooo"

He started running and as he ran the little green figures ran in all different directions. Nugget didn't see the tree limb that must have fallen since he passed earlier. His foot caught on it and he fell with a loud crash and thud. His leg twisted and his head hit a rock. He didn't move or utter a sound.

CHAPTER TWENTY-NINE

The Kin were close, by as they only had time to hide, when they heard Nugget yell. The Dubars had taken but a couple minutes to prepare to leave, even though they all figured it wasn't necessary to rush. Now each in his separate hiding place wondered why Nugget was back. They didn't worry for they were all good at hiding from Toobigs but no one wanted to move until Nugget stood so they would know what he would do.

When ten minutes passed and Nugget never moved, Dodo knew something was wrong. He left his hiding place and walked over to Nugget. He saw the man was unconscious and his head was bleeding. On further inspection it looked like he had a broken arm and leg. Dodo motioned to the others to come from hiding and he joined them a little distance from Nugget.

Dodo decided he must take over and make decisions and everyone agreed. The Kin lived by the rule of helping all people in need so they could not leave now. They must help Nugget. Dodo knew they needed Doc's help and fast. The Kin could take care of the wound and they knew how to set bones, but Nugget needed to be moved indoors and that they could not do. Dodo said Timmy should try to call Aquila and send a message to Doc and Joe telling them they were needed because Nugget was injured. Suzy and Kestrel should also come. Suma and Kale were to go back to the village and lead them here. Dodo didn't want Nugget to see any more Kin as he may start wondering how many little people there were. Nugget had seen Dodo, Suzy and Kestrel with Doc and he just thought of them as Doc's kids. By kidnapping only Timmy they figured Nugget thought only Timmy and the Dubars were unique.

Suma and Kale took off running, using Nuggets trail it made travel out of Night Forest much easier. They found it led to a path they recognized because of trees that Kin had marked on some previous journey. Now they could make good time.

After Suma and Kale left, Timmy located Aquila and gave him the message for help. Dodo and the Dubars went to work.

Tish built up the fire in the stove and put water on to heat. Bern and Timmy took blankets and covered Nugget to keep him warm. Dodo got clean cloth and shears from Tish and taking some of the water, which was barely warm, he ran back out to Nugget. Very carefully he trimmed all of Nuggets beard away from the wounds and washed them thoroughly. He bound clean dry cloth over the cuts after cleaning but there wasn't any thing else to do but wait for Doc.

Dodo was gently lifting Nugget's head to place a pillow under it when Nugget roused and looking up into Dodo's face he asked what had happened. Dodo explained he had tripped and fell and was badly hurt with broken bones. Nugget took a moment to remember. When he did he realized why he had been running, but then why were they still here. He couldn't figure it out so he asked Dodo. Dodo had discarded his green cap and shirt top so Nugget only saw his plaid shirt he had worn under the jacket. He didn't want to appear as more than a friend to Timmy. Dodo told him it was not his way to leave an injured person and not the way of Timmy's friends, so they all stayed. Nugget, remembering Doc, asked where Doc and the rest of his family were. Dodo replied that they were camped in the woods and would be there as soon as Timmy could get them. Nugget hadn't seen Timmy so at Dodos words he went into hiding until Doc would arrive.

Nugget lay quietly. He soon thought of the fishing trip he had started on and now poor Iggy Wando was tied up and waiting with no food or water. It was only noon, but he didn't think of that, just about his donkey alone. He looked at Dodo, who was checking the bandage and asked if he would go get his donkey. He told Dodo about where to find Iggy Wondo. Dodo consented and left Tish and Bern to watch over the injured man.

Dodo found Timmy sitting by the trail out of sight of Nugget's home. He walked along with Dodo until they found the donkey. Timmy greeted his four legged friend and communicated what had happened. Timmy remained out of sight when they returned. Dodo took the pack off the animal and then put him in his little shed or barn as the Dubars called it. Nugget nodded his approval.

The afternoon seemed to pass very slowly. Nugget didn't want to eat but often asked for water and would question why they were helping him after what he had done. He seemed to think they had an unknown reason for staying and helping him. These were Timmy's friends and not thieves as he had first believed and he just couldn't believe these people were so good.

Evening was approaching and it was getting a little cold so Dodo built a bon-fire. The moon shone brightly and this plus Doc's flashlight, Dodo hoped, would keep Doc and Joe from stopping for the night.

Timmy had sneaked back to the house and he and his parents were resting.

It was about midnight when Doc and Joe came rushing into the yard. Dodo met him a ways from Nugget and Doc whispered that Suma was around the bend and Kale was with Suzy and Kestrel who were traveling slower. He asked Dodo to see to Suma who was very tired.

Doc and Joe went over to Nugget and Doc examined him. First he looked Over Nugget's wounds finding Dodo had done a fine job of cleaning them, but Doc wanted to spread antibiotic on them. He opened his medical bag, which he always carried and Nugget awoke as Doc was checking it. Nugget groaned but gave no greeting. Doc then checked his arm and leg. The leg was definitely broken but the arm he decided had just been badly sprained at the shoulder. By now Timmy and the Dubars were awake and after a quick hug, at the reunion, Doc asked if they had anything to fashion strips of cloth for binding. The Dubars found an old sheet and Doc tore it into strips to bind the arm to Nuggets side. He had sent Joe to find or make splints for the leg. Joe knew what he wanted and he soon returned with what was needed. After giving pain medication to Nugget, Doc set and bound the leg.

"Now," Doc said, "comes the hard part, getting him into bed."

It was quite a dilemma. Everyone had suggestions, even Nugget, but Timmy became the hero. His idea was to get the donkey, then help Nugget to stand on his good foot and then he could lay across the animals back. As the door was wide enough, the donkey could carry him into the house and right to his bed. Everyone, even Nugget, approved of this and soon he was safely in his bed.

It was now about two in the morning, everyone wanted to sleep but Timmy. Kestrel and Suzy had arrived shortly after Nugget got to bed and now Timmy wanted to talk. He wanted to know everything that had happened and where they had been since he was kidnapped.

Doc told Timmy, "No way, you can talk all day tomorrow."

Everyone was happy to hear Doc's comment to Timmy. After finding nooks and corners to curl up within, soon all were asleep.

The next morning Doc and Joe stayed in the cabin discussing the situation. All the others went outside where Nugget couldn't hear them or see them from his window. Kestrel could now hug her old friends Tish and Bern and say how much they had been missed. She introduced her niece Suzy. They of course knew about Suzy from Timmy's story.

Suma and Kale joined them and Suzy asked Timmy to tell what had happened after he was kidnapped. When he was done she would relate where they had been.

Timmy said he didn't have much to tell but he made a story of his journey making the trip through the mine tunnel seem scary and spooky. He concluded by saying how wonderful it had been to see his parents but how boring it had been to stay in the cabin day after day.

"Boring, boring, boring," Timmy repeated.

"Oh Timmy," Suzy said, "it hasn't been but about two weeks."

"But it seems like a year," Timmy exclaimed." He continued, "I can hardly wait to get home and see everyone and have some fun and I don't want to miss the fall festival. Oh, I know I can't be seen this year in Mini Creek, but I think I've found a new way to be there. I found a book Nugget has, and I have been studying it. If it works, boy will I be flying high." He stopped talking abruptly as though he had said too much, but added "Your turn Suzy."

Suzy told about everything they had done and seen. She finished by telling Dodo that Jeb had finished carving the words on the statue base and it was beautiful. Now all we have to do is plan how to get it to the jeep.

Timmy was again quick to solve the question.

"My friend Nugget's donkey of course," he said, and added, "And I should go along as he knows me. Maybe we can go tomorrow."

All during Suzy's story he had wondered how he could get to see this other Kin village before going home. When Dodo said his idea was the only solution he was too happy to speak. He knew his parents would okay it. Now he had to hope Doc would.

Doc and Joe had been deciding what should be done. Doc said he would like to get everyone back home at least by the middle of August. It was well into July now and it would take six weeks for Nuggets leg to heal, if all went well. They couldn't leave Nugget alone and he had said he wouldn't go to Skagway. He would make it somehow. Joe thought about everything that was said and then he told Doc he would stay until Nugget was well. Doc hated to put this burden on Joe but Joe said he was ready for a vacation in the woods and some fishing. Joe nodded toward the door then and they walked out.

Out of Nuggets hearing Joe said, "I know you didn't want Nugget to know of your new friends, but maybe they could secretly stop and check with me. I'm sure I'll do fine but I may need help with fishing or something."

Doc replied, "A great idea, I will arrange it and now I won't feel we left you alone with the injured man.

Joe went back inside and Doc went to tell his daughter and friends.

Everything was soon arranged. Timmy and Dodo would take the donkey and go with Suma and Kale to the village. From the village they would go directly to the jeep with the statue. Then

Timmy would bring the donkey to Nuggets where the rest would be waiting to leave. Dodo would stay at the jeep. They were told not to hurry because Doc wanted a couple more days to be sure Nuggets wounds were healing.

All went as planned. The second day Timmy came back with the donkey. Everyone was ready to leave and had bid Nugget and Joe goodbye. As they waited Timmy put the donkey in the barn and as he put his arms around his neck said, "I'll miss you Iggy Wando." He saw a tear roll down the donkey's cheek.

Timmy than ran into the cabin, picked up a book and went into Nugget's room. He went close to the bed and he said, "Mr. Nugget sir, I have come to say goodbye. I will probably never see you again, so I can't borrow this book so if you don't read it anymore I was wondering if I could have it, because there are things in this book that make me think I could maybe fly and then I will always have something to remember you by."

As usual when excited Timmy had talked without a pause and rather jumbled up his words.

Nugget looked at Timmy and smiled at him for the first time, as he said, "Yes, Timmy I give it to you to keep, I will always remember you and will imagine you flying. I am sorry for kidnapping you and your friends but I do know you have all changed my life. I was mixed up in my thinking and believed you were spies hunting for me. Now I know better and I think that Bern and Tish are your parents. Not just friends, am I right?"

Timmy nodded, "Yes."

Nugget continued, "I realized that a few days ago and was trying to find an answer to what I should do but now your friends have made it right. I want you and your parents to know that when I was running to the house and yelled nooo, just before I fell, it was because I was afraid the ones running out of my house had probably hurt you and your folks. If I had known they were friends I would have just let you all go. I just hope you can all forgive me."

Timmy felt so good hearing these words that he stood on his tip toes and leaned over and hugged Nugget, as he said, "Of course we forgive you."

Tears were in Nuggets eyes, but Timmy didn't see them, as he ran from the room.

The party was ready to leave. Joe walked with them to the bend in the path and as they turned the corner the surprise they got was overwhelming. It seemed at least half the Yukon Kin village had come this far to say their goodbyes. Jeb, the carver was with them and he gave a small carved animal to each. He said he had given Dodo a deer earlier. Now Suzy got a bear, Timmy an eagle and Kestrel a small replica of the statue. It just seemed too much. There was laughing, crying and hugs as each group finally knew it was time to part.

Aquila had been waiting with Dodo at the jeep for he was eager to see his old friends Tish and Bern, after so many years. Tish and Bern laughed and cried with happiness when they saw the dear eagle who watched and worried over their son years ago.

CHAPTER THIRTY

After the jeep was packed and ready to go, Aquila flew off and then Timmy yelled, "Skagway, here we come."

Much to Timmy's disappointment the trip down from White Pass was uneventful.

Doc went to see Jake at his store and thanked him for all his help and asked if he would keep the jeep at his place and give it to Joe when he got back. He explained where Joe was and said everything turned out fine. The jeep was Doc's gift to Joe.

Doc next went to the airport where he had left his party and baggage and hired a plane to take them to Juneau. By night they were on a ferry headed for Seattle.

Aquila had almost lost them. He watched them get on the plane, saw the direction it was headed, but certainly couldn't keep up. He knew it was toward Seattle so he flew south. When he reached Juneau and was flying over, he saw the plane. Due to Doc and party having to wait for the ferry, he had arrived in time to see them board. He now knew they were going home and he was a happy bird.

Doc had managed to get two cabins on the ferry but it wasn't luxurious like the cruise ship. Some people even put small tents up and slept on the deck.

The day after boarding the ferry, Timmy, carrying the book from Nugget, found a place on deck and started looking at the drawings in it. He stopped after a couple hours and was idly flipping the pages when a thin clipping dropped out. He had just finished reading it when Dodo came looking for him to say it was lunchtime. Timmy jumped up to go with Dodo, for he could hardly wait to tell what he now knew.

When everyone was busy eating Timmy broke the silence with his news. "I know who Nugget is."

Everyone looked up and as one they said, "What?"

"I know who Nugget is", he repeated. "He is the Great Korineski."

When Timmy said no more Suzy spoke up, "Timmy" she said, "If you really have something to say, then say it or skip it and don't try to be dramatic all the time. Who is Korineski?"

Timmy replied, "But it is dramatic. This fell out of the book Nugget gave me. Wait until you hear."

He held up a newspaper clipping from an Anchorage paper dated ten years ago. He handed the paper to Doc to read aloud. It said that Korineski was a great Russian magician and he was to perform in the theater in Anchorage on June first but he never appeared. He had been looked for and many inquires had been made but six month later he still had not been located. There was a picture of him and it looked much like Nugget had.

Doc put the paper down and said, "I think you are right Timmy and it explains why he was upset that Dodo cut off his beard and why he was suspicious of people. Well, now we know who he is but we will never know why he chose to change his life. I think it best we keep his secret. May I see the book Timmy?"

Timmy handed him the book and Doc explained, "This is written in Russian."

"I know," said Timmy, "but Nugget said it was about flying and he knew I would like to fly and I liked the sketches. I didn't tell him, but I thought maybe Professor Vanir could read it."

Doc replied, "Timmy, I know a little Russian and this book is called "The Magic of Flying, but it is really a book about magic. Yes I'm sure Professor Vanir will be able to read it. It is a nice gift Nugget gave you." Doc then gave the book back to Timmy.

Timmy spent the rest of the day dreaming of all the magic he may be able to learn from his book if only Professor Vanir would teach him Russian. Maybe he wouldn't be able to fly but then again maybe magic could make it possible.

The following day Orcas were again seen and Timmy was tempted to jump overboard, for he was sure the whales would help him. He looked up and saw Aquila fly past overhead. He had the feeling Aquila knew what he was thinking because as he started to climb the railing, he heard a loud screech and he knew it was a warning from Aquila. He backed away from the railing, saying to himself, "Someday I'll ride on an Orca."

That night they reached Seattle. Doc called a cab and took everyone to his Seattle home. He would liked to have gone on to the Kin village but knowing they were probably tired and curious to see what his house was like he decided to stay until the next night.

Narvik was overjoyed at learning they had found the Dubars and grabbed his old friends Tish and Bern in a big hug. He was dying to hear their story but said he would wait until they reached home so they wouldn't have to repeat it.

CHAPTER THIRTY-ONE

The next night Doc took them home to their village. Aquila had flown in early and informed Professor Vanir they were on the way and the Dubars were with them. The Kin went in to a whirlwind of activity, fixing welcome banners and creating a feast. When the travelers arrived the village held the biggest celebration ever and it was a wonderful surprise for the Dubars. Happiness was in every ones heart but Granny Dubar seemed happiest of all.

After eating and telling of all their adventures, Dodo said they would now reveal the gift they had brought back for the Toobigs of Mini Creek. This caused much whispering and questions, as how could they give a whole town a gift secretly. Dodo and Doc lifted the wrapped statue out of the trunk. Everyone was mystified by its size. Dodo took the wrapping off and there was complete silence wondering what it was all about, until someone read the words at the base. "Who Knows". Some of the Kin still didn't know but the younger ones did and they hooted and clapped. Then Woody, Dodo, Hoot, Chuck, Dawn, Fern, Bebe, Phin and Timmy joined hands and made a circle dancing around the statue while Kestrel explained what the young folks planned.

The celebrations were coming to an end when Timmy jumped upon a bench and said he would like to make a request.

The gathering people shouted, "Okay Timmy, what is it?"

Timmy replied, "Well, as you all know Suzy asked us to drop the Q from her name, I would now like to be called Tim. Timmy was okay for Mini Creek but now I have a new life."

As Timmy stepped back down the whole village responded with, "Hooray for Tim."

CHAPTER THIRTY-TWO

It was the first of August and all the Kin were working to make things for the Mini Creek Fall Festival. They liked to see the Toobigs exclaim over their hand made items and carvings. It was fun being among the Toobigs, with the Toobigs never knowing whom they were talking to.

Kestrel and Suzy showed how the Kin up north had used shells, fern, pebbles and reeds in their artwork and many were now trying new ideas for wall plaques. Tim spent most of his time with Professor Vanir who was teaching him Russian.

The days seemed to pass way too quickly for the young Kin, for they couldn't decide on how to get the statue to Mini Creek. They wanted to secretly put it in the town square the last night of the festival. It seemed a good night for everyone usually locked up their business and went to the festival.

Ten days before the festival Doc went to Mini Creek. He wanted to check on his house there and to meet with James (Jingles), Bender and Maria. He had written to them that all was ready for them in Seattle. He would take them to the ferry and they would be met in Seattle. By time they were settled in their new home he would be back in Seattle and help them enroll at the university. While they were saying goodbye to friends he said he wanted to talk to the druggist. He really had another reason for going into Mini Creek. He wanted to walk around the town square and look for a place for the Kin's statue. He thought their idea was unusual and great fun and he wanted to help. The town would have a wonderful mystery for years to come if it could be done right.

He stopped at the drugstore after viewing the town square and asked how the festival preparations were going.

The druggist said, "Doc haven't you heard? Oh, that's right, you have been gone for a month. Well things aren't so good, a bunch of kids are camped out some where near and every day they come in town and take over the park. They don't do anything illegal but they act like bullies and are very threatening to our people. Some out of towner's came early to start setting up their sales booths and the next morning something is always smashed or boards and other things are missing. Doc, I don't know if there will be a festival. We think those boys are doing the damage but we can't prove it, and people are getting worried. Town people thought the out of towner's were exaggerating so they spent all day yesterday building a nice stage. Mini Creek wants to put on a musical this year and make some money for the school kids. Well this morning it was all torn down. Have you got any ideas Doc? I sure wish there really was a "Who Knows!"

Doc was really upset on hearing the bad news and said, "Well, I'll see if I can come up with an idea, but I doubt it. I feel terrible and I had wanted to bring some youngsters here from Seattle again this year. I have to go now and take James, Bender and Maria to the ferry. I'll see you later."

"I heard about what you are doing Doc, and the town folks think its great. Good luck and check back, it may come out all right so you can bring the youngsters."

Doc took the three young people to the ferry and after they were safely aboard he drove back to his house. He checked everything to be sure it would be ready for the Kin. He wanted them to stay there whenever they wished. The garage and its private room was a safe place for the Kin to rest and hide within. At dusk he left for The Ham.

He waited until morning to tell a gathering of Suzy's friends about the trouble at Mini Creek. When he ended talking by saying the druggist had said he wished there really was a "Who Knows", they knew it was a job for the Kin. They had to get rid of the Toobig teens and save the festival. The town Toobigs putting on a musical was bound to empty the town of everyone and give the Kin time to install the statue.

Everyone came up with wild ideas of ways to get rid of the teens, but none were very good. Tim thought he should ask Professor Vanir as they needed some big help.

Professor Vanir listened as Tim told him everything that was going on in Mini Creek. Tim had told the Professor about the statue when he had told him of his adventure in Alaska. Professor Vanir had not commented about it, but he was like Doc, secretly tickled over it. He knew he must help. Professor Vanir didn't respond for several minutes, then he said "Come and see me tomorrow at lunch, I may have a solution for your problem.

Tim went back to his friends and told them what Professor Vanir had said. Knowing the Professor was working on their problem was a big relief but waiting until tomorrow seemed to take forever.

Tim was at Professor Vanir's door promptly at noon. He looked over at the huge stump where Aquila usually perched. Aquila was there but sitting beside him was a very large owl and at the base of the stump was the biggest mountain lion that Tim had ever seen. He stood motionless staring. The Professor stepped out and took his hand and led him to the creatures, telling Tim they were all very old friends of his, and between them they had reached a plan to truly frighten the Toobig teen bullies. Tim could call them Owl and Leo. Tim was told to come back around dusk and to be wearing his hidey clothes. He would then be told what he and the Profs' animal friends were to do. He could also tell his friends it would be taken care of tonight and they would be told tomorrow how it was done.

Tim returned to Professor Vanir's that evening. The Professor told Tim that he, Owl and Leo had visited the camp of the Toobig teen bullies the previous evening. Owl had been perched on Leo's back and Leo awoke the Toobig teen bullies by growling loudly. They screamed and scrambled into their car, which was parked right by their sleeping bags.

Professor Vanir issued a stern warning from where he was hid, but it sounded as though Owl was speaking. He had said, "These streams and mountains belong to us. This is to warn you, leave and do not return or we will cause you much harm."

Professor Vanir had seen they were really scared but after they locked themselves in the car they seemed less worried. They laughed, and didn't drive away so The Prof, Leo and Owl left. Aquila stayed to see what they would do. This morning they hurriedly collected theirs sleeping bags and moved over by the park. The Prof said it seemed they would have to try again. He told Tim his plan and Tim was eager to follow instructions, as he loved adventures and this seemed like a good one.

Tim, doing as he was told left The Ham seated on Leos back. His weight was no problem for Leo and Leo loped through the forest. Tim clung to his fur to keep from falling. Owl and Aquila were flying overhead. Shortly two other mountain lions joined them and they continued on to the park. They located the Toobig teen bullies camp, and when they saw the boys were still up they hid in the bushes and waited. The Toobig teen bullies were talking and laughing as they sat around the campfire. As they listened they heard them arguing whether what happened the night before was a prank by the villagers or what else could have happened. Two of the Toobig teen bullies wanted to leave but the other three called them sissies.

One of the Toobig teen boys who wanted to leave said, "No one can convince me that was some ones stunt. Animals don't talk and the forest is their home. I'm telling you all, since the car is mine, if anything like last night happens again I'm leaving and going back to Seattle with or without any of you."

Tim having heard all they said could hardly wait for them to go to sleep so his fun could begin.

The Toobig teen bullies were now grumbling about scared babies and nothing would happen and they wouldn't miss the festival. The owner of the car paid no attention and crawled into his sleeping bag. The others soon did the same. In a half an hour all was quiet.

Tim waited a while longer and then all took their places. Aquila and Owl perched on the car top. One lion leaped up on the hood and one stood by the car doors so the Toobigs would see there was no escape. Tim seated himself on Leo's back and dressed completely in green he looked like a very small Peter Pan.

Leo strolled over to the sleeping bag of the teen who had spoke the meanest words and gave him a big wet sloppy lick across his face.

The boy thought one of the other boys was pulling a joke and without opening his eyes, he yelled, "Cut it out."

This woke all the others who were sleeping lightly, still nervous from the night before. One teen sat up and looked around and started screeching. The meanest teen opened his eyes and stared into Leo's eyes and the huge tongue just inches from his face. The teens nearest the car were struggling to get out of their bags and then saw the lions by the car. Now truly frightened the boys didn't know which way to turn. The scene before their eyes was truly unbelievable, and they stayed frozen to the spot. With only the light from the moon they saw no way out.

Leo now stepped back a few feet and Tim spoke as a ventriloquist so the Toobig teen bullies thought it was Owl speaking, "Last night you were warned! You didn't believe. Now we have a problem about your punishment. We will have to take you deep into the forest and let the mountain creatures decide your fate. It may be bad because you didn't heed last nights warning. You will follow Leo, our king. We others will walk behind you, but beware, many others in these mountains will also watch you, you can not escape."

Tim paused so the teens had time to understand what had been said. The boys were no longer blustering and laughing they were crying and shaking with fear. Looking toward the Owl the boys started sobbing the words "Please, please, please!"

Tim had a hard time keeping from laughing. Once again he spoke, "You bullies almost seem sorry. I will give one of you one chance to plead why you should not be punished. Then as I am first judge in the King's Court I will decide whether to let you go or to take you up the mountain to the full court."

The young car owner, visibly trembling, spoke, "Your honor, we are in the wrong, I am truly sorry, the others will do as they will, but I will bully no more. If you let me go I will get in my car and leave the Olympic peninsula and never come back. I will take the others with me if they feel the same and want to go. Thank you."

Tim could tell the one who spoke was truly sincere. He wasn't sure about all of them but they did all say they agreed. He thought it best not to answer too fast but let them think old Owl was trying to decide.

When Tim believed they had been frightened long enough he spoke, "I have decided. You all may go, but if you ever return you will not be let go again. We will watch you pack and leave and follow you."

The Toobig teen bullies started falling all over each other in their haste to grab their belongings. They then scrambled to throw their things and themselves into the car. The driver couldn't find his car keys and jumped back out of the car, frantically clawing the dirt in an attempt to find them. At last he found them, leapt into the car, ground the motor trying to start the car, finally getting it started he floored the gas and fishtailed out of the camp sight.

Aquila was instructed to fly overhead and swoop down where the Toobig teen bullies could see him from the car, so they would know they were being followed.

Tim thanked Owl and the lions and they went their way. Leo took Tim home where Professor Vanir waited. When the Prof learned all was well he sent Leo to his den and he and Tim went to bed.

Tim had a wonderful time the next day telling his friends about the Toobig teen bullies departure. Everyone always enjoyed hearing of his actions whenever he was called on to help. His description of his words as a judge and the Toobig teen bullies believing it, was extremely funny to Tim's friends. They all congratulated him on his success in getting rid of the Toobig teen bullies.

CHAPTER THRITY-THREE

Two days before the festival the Kin packed Doc's truck. They put in all they needed for three days plus the things they made to sell and the statue. Dodo, Chuck and Dawn were to work the booth. This year Suzy would have to stay hidden but she and Tim couldn't bear to be left out. No one could say no since they were staying with Suzy's father. Narvik also went to help with the statue. Doc drove the truck and Kin to his house in the evening.

The next day Doc, Dodo, Chuck and Dawn left for the park. Doc stopped by the drug store first.

When Doc went in the store he greeted the druggist with, "Hi, how are things in town?'

"Fine," said the druggist, "The bad boys are gone. No one knows when, but they haven't been seen for some days now. Why? Well as the town people say, "Who Knows"?

Doc replied, "Sure glad to hear that, now my young friends can set up a booth. Well, see you later."

Doc went back to the truck and as he drove the Kin to the park he told them what the druggist had said. Dodo was especially happy about hearing the comment and hoped all went well in placing the statue.

Doc and the three spent the afternoon building their booth. Tomorrow they would come into town early to arrange their items for sale.

Doc and his three young companions returned to Doc's house late in the afternoon. Dodo rushed out to the garage to tell Suzy and Tim about the day's happenings. It had really been hard on Suzy and Tim to stay inside all day so Dodo's visit was very welcome.

That evening they all gathered in the house with the shades drawn tight. After having a nice dinner Doc said he had some ideas and wanted to know if everyone wished to hear them or had they already decided on how to place the statue. They all wanted to hear Doc's ideas because they didn't know what to do.

Doc said, "As you know tomorrow may not be too busy as people arrive and walk about looking at what is for sale and then buying, we hope. So we shouldn't plan moving the statue. I'm not going to say Suzy and Tim have to stay in tomorrow night but if they sneak over to the park they better be dressed in their green hidey clothes and stay well hidden. The next day, Saturday, will be different. There will probably be a lot more people and it will be busy at the park. I understand all the businesses will close at six o'clock. The ads for the town musical show, have asked all those who have booths to have everything packed up at ten minutes to ten. The show will then start at ten and everyone can see it and not have to watch their booths. When I was in town earlier, I saw where the statue should go. There is a concrete base, about two feet high, in the center of the town square. It is the perfect length and width. It was once part of a fountain and when it was broken the town left the base, hoping to someday have money to replace the fountain. There is a large bunch of lilac bushes off to one side and I was thinking Narvik and I could stay home, until almost ten, before we go to get the stuff from the booth. Then on the way I would stop for a few minutes and Suzy and Tim, who would be under tarps, could jump out and hide in the bushes while Narvik put the statue there also. I would then drive to the park and get our things and we would see the show, while Suzy, Tim and Narvik place the statue. Everyone should be in the park by then and if anyone sees Narvik, well the people here know he has worked for me for years and wouldn't connect him to the statue. Now questions anyone?"

Tim said he had one. When he lived in Mini Creek he said there was always this big spotlight turned on at night in the town square and he worried about that, if anyone should be around. Doc asked if he had ever seen it turned on or if he knew where the switch was. He said he wasn't sure but it might be in a box on the side of the sheriff's office because he sort of remembered the light coming on at the same time the Sheriff had lifted the cover. He also heard the Sheriff say he wished the town would fix it so he wouldn't always have to remember it.

Doc said he thought Tim was probably right.

Dodo exclaimed, "Hey, that would be great if Tim is right. Narvik could turn it off. It would just seem it was forgotten if anyone came while they were setting the statue in place."

It was agreed. Doc's idea was as good as possible so they decided to get some sleep.

Friday the day went fast for those at the festival. For Suzy and Tim it seemed night would never arrive. At last it was dark enough for them to leave the garage. Suzy was very excited and really enjoying the game of 'Don't be seen by Toobigs.' Suzy was good at traveling unseen but Tim was even better and Suzy watched him and learned. When they got to the park it was fun seeing old school mates. They were in their green suits and managed to work their way under a large bunch of rhododendron bushes. Their friends had told them where their booth was and now they were near it. They had a perfect hiding place and had just got settled when to their surprise they saw Veronica, without her mother. She was with two girls Suzy knew from school. Veronica handled everything and made rude comments making her friends laugh. She pointed to a carving of a bear and said it was simply dreadful. Phin had spent hours carving the bear and. Tim knew it was perfect. Veronica picked up the figure and was making fun of the bears shape.

The bear replied in a whisper "It's nicer than yours."

Of course it was Tim doing his voice trick, because he was so upset with Veronica's remarks. Those who had heard tried not to laugh, but a few giggles were heard. Veronica thought one of her friends had made the remark and she was near tears.

Veronica stood for some time holding the small figure of the bear, then she quietly said, "I will buy it."

Tim and Suzy had expected her to react like she had last year and were very surprised at her behavior.

Veronica's friends were also surprised.

One friend said, "Why on earth would you buy that ugly thing?"

Veronica picked up her purchase and as she turned away Tim and Suzy just barely heard her soft murmur, "To remind me to be kinder."

Tim looked at Suzy and said that now he felt bad for saying what he had. Suzy told him she didn't think he should for it sounded like Veronica was trying to behave better and so Tim had probably helped her.

Then Suzy said, "I think we should just say it was help from 'Who Knows'."

Suzy's remark made Tim feel better and they enjoyed the rest of the evening in hiding until time to go back to Doc's.

Saturday was another beautiful sunny day and Suzy and Tim hated spending it in the room in the garage. Tim spent the morning studying Russian and then spent the afternoon telling Suzy how great next year would be. He was learning magic and hoped to do wonderful and mysterious things by next year. He also told Suzy he had a new feathered friend. During the time he spent at Professor Vanir's he had found a big crow perched on a low branch. The crow's wing had been injured and he had asked Suzy's Dad to bandage it. While it was healing he had been teaching it to talk. It now knew several words.

"Just think," Tim said, "how much he will add to our Halloween fun. I have been keeping the crow and my magic learning sort of a secret but I wanted to tell my best friend, you of course, and ask for help in naming the crow."

"Oh Tim," Suzy replied, "I am so proud to be called your best friend and to help think of a name. Let's see if we can decide on one before we go out tonight."

Suzy and Tim wondered aloud where to get a name. Suzy was thinking about things she had learned in school and asked Tim if he remembered studying about the Native American Crow people. Tim became excited and said of course he did. Now all they needed was a crow name.

Finally Suzy said, "Let's call him Sioux. I remember in the book I read that was the main name for many different Crow Tribes. They all had great leaders and I bet your crow does great things.

This pleased Tim and he said, "So he shall be named Sioux."

Evening had arrived and after dinner Suzy and Tim could hardly sit still. Every ten minutes they looked at the clock. Then the time was nine thirty and it was time to climb in the truck bed and hide with the statue.

Doc drove slowly toward the town square. When he arrived it seemed everyone had left just as he had expected. He stopped near the lilac and stepped out but he wasn't as lucky as he thought. Someone called his name.

"Hey Doc, what's the trouble? You are going to be late for the show. Need some help?" It was the druggist, standing by his car.

Doc hurriedly replied, "No everything is fine. Just checking my tires. You go ahead I'll be there in a jiffy."

The druggist left and Narvik, Tim and Suzy jumped out. They unloaded the statue and a jar of glue. Doc got back in the truck and told Narvik he should wait a few minutes before turning off the town square light.

Narvik waited a little, then walked toward the Sheriff's office. Hoping Tim was right about where the switch was; he remembered to stay in the shadows just in case someone was still in the town center. When he reached, where Tim had told him to go, he saw the box. He opened it, found a switch and flipped it and as the big light went off it remained quiet, so he was sure everyone was gone. He raced back to the town center to where the statue was. He and Tim picked it up and carried it to the old fountain base. Tim knew just where to find it in the faint light from the street lamps for he had played here, as had Suzy, when living with the Haveahordes. The glue Suzy was carrying was because of an idea from her father. He had used the permanent glue to fasten the statue to the carved name base. As the statue wasn't big or very heavy he thought it should be fastened solidly to the concrete and all agreed. Suzy liberally smeared the concrete with glue and Narvik and Tim set the statue in place. They waited until the glue had begun to stick well. It had only taken about thirty minutes.

Narvik said, "Give me the glue jar Suzy and lets run for it."

Suzy handed him the jar, which he stuck in his pocket and she said, "What do you mean, run for it, were done here. We don't have to hurry."

Narvik replied, "Don't you want to see the show? If we really run we should only miss the first half hour."

Suzy and Tim had only been thinking of the statue and knew they would have to miss the musical. They had told each other they didn't mind, but when Narvik said what he did, they laughed and away they ran toward the park. As they left, Narvik switched the light back on and thought how lucky for all, the statue placing went so well.

Doc had thought if all went well they may run to the park, so when the Kin packed up what little they hadn't sold, he had them take the booth down too. He parked the truck where the booth had been which gave a good view of the stage.

Narvik, Suzy and Tim reached the park just as the mayor, visiting guests and others had finished their welcome speeches and the main show was about to begin. All eyes were on the stage so Tim and Suzy climbed into the back of Doc's truck and pulled a tarp over themselves. All that showed was a bump in the tarp, below which their eyes peered out. Narvik got in the front. They were so glad they got there to see the show. When it ended Suzy and Tim hid their faces.

Doc, Dawn, Dodo and Chuck came back to the truck and the three Kin climbed into the back.

Suzy whispered, "Don't sit on us."

Doc heard the laughing and knew where his daughter and Tim were, and without Narvik telling him.

The town people were leaving the park now. Some of them were walking. Doc drove slow and stopped on Main Street to let the crowd cross as some of the families, who were walking, decided to take a short cut through the town square. They had barely entered when there were shouts from several people. The Sheriff and everyone that heard ran to the town square. They hurried to where others were standing and saw what caused the shouts.

There was total amazement. After the first shouts everyone stood silently and stared.

Doc, Narvik, Dawn, Chuck and Dodo had left the truck and were now standing among the silent crowd. Suzy and Tim had managed, due to all the excitement, to leave the truck and hide in the lilac bushes.

The silence continued for several minutes, then there were murmurs of how, why, when? It was as though no one dared speak loudly.

Finally Granny Nelson, whose apples had been secretly picked and boxed last year, came forward and stood by the statue. She raised her hands for silence and in as loud a voice as she could manage said, "So, now at last we know what "Who Knows" looks like. I think it's time we give "Who Knows" a great heartfelt thank you with a shout and much applause."

The response was tremendous!

The end

Printed in the United States
25613LVS00001B/420